Praise fo

'A modern classic of children's fantasy
with a necessary hero'

– Lizzie Huxley-Jones,
author of the *Vivi Conway* series

'I loved this book – a triumphant and richly
imagined fantasy as well as a compelling insight
into life with seizures and memory loss'

– Lee Newbery,
author of *The Last Firefox* series

'Funny, heart-warming and imaginative voyage
into memory, meaning and identity'

– BookTrust

'Imaginative . . . this is a hopeful fantasy
adventure with a brave and kind young hero'

– The Week Junior

'Spend the Easter holidays lost in a mystery'

– First News

JAYBEN

AND THE
STAR GLASS

THOMAS LEEDS

HODDER CHILDREN'S BOOKS

First published in Great Britain in 2024 by Hodder & Stoughton

1 3 5 7 9 10 8 6 4 2

Text copyright © Thomas Leeds, 2024
Illustration copyright © Teo Skaffa, 2024

The moral rights of the author and illustrator have been asserted.

A CIP catalogue record for this book is available
from the British Library.

ISBN 978 1 444 96866 8

Typeset in Sabon by Palimpsest Book Production Limited,
Falkirk, Stirlingshire

Printed and bound in Great Britain by Clays Ltd, Elcograf S.p.A.

The paper and board used in this book
are made from wood from responsible sources.

MIX
Paper | Supporting
responsible forestry
FSC® C104740

Hodder Children's Books
An imprint of
Hachette Children's Group
Part of Hodder & Stoughton Limited
Carmelite House
50 Victoria Embankment
London EC4Y 0DZ

An Hachette UK Company
www.hachette.co.uk

www.hachettechildrens.co.uk

For Sophie, Phoebe,
Lucy and my parents,
Jacqueline and Tony.

In memory of my wonderful
English tutor, Angela Myers.

And for every child who is living
with an illness or a disability.
Whatever your story,
you can be the hero.

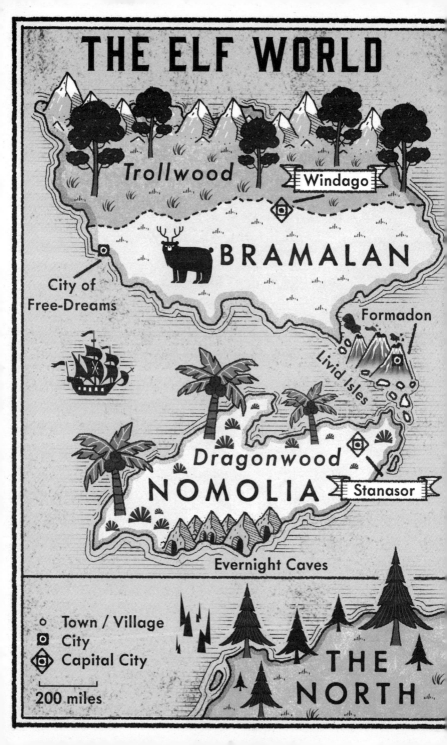

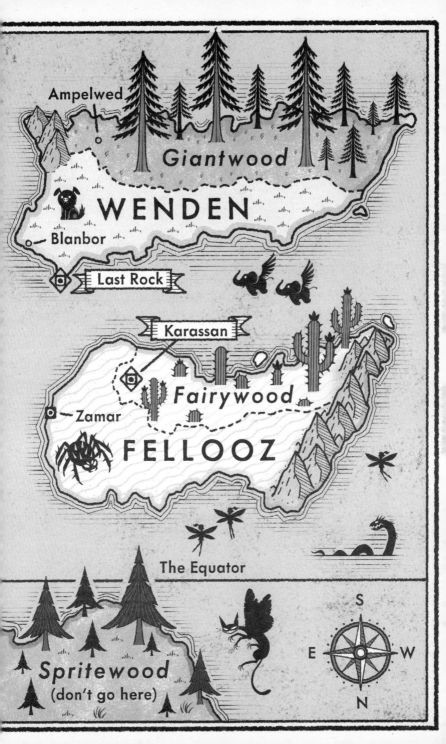

Ampelwed

Giantwood

WENDEN

Blanbor

Last Rock

Karassan

Fairywood

Zamar

FELLOOZ

The Equator

Spritewood
(don't go here)

S

E   W

N

CHAPTER 1

Alone on Christmas Eve

Storms of ice raged in a world far away. A world in which nobody dreamed but for one powerful child, who was sound asleep, and one adult who was thirsty for revenge.

A masked figure in a grey fur cloak paced inside the empty dining car of a train as it sped through a moonlit forest. Two armed men entered from the next carriage, carrying something under a cloth that glowed green. The figure stopped pacing. Tiny black dragons emerged from under the seats, blowing sparks and pecking each other with their razor-sharp beaks as they jostled for the green glow.

The men removed the cloth to reveal a mirror with

a frame of gleaming emeralds. In the glass, the face of a man appeared. He had an orange tan, short black hair and a chunky gold necklace on his bare chest.

'We found it!' the man shouted. He showed off a yellow gem. 'The tomb full of star glass!'

'Very good, Zamar,' said the figure from behind the expressionless white porcelain mask.

'You'll get your power back,' the man continued excitedly. 'With the solar eclipse, these gems will make you *three times* stronger.'

'Yes. And once our Agents have found the Torch—' The figure stopped, distracted, and looked out of the train window. There were lines of bright lights in the night sky, beneath the full moon. 'The lights? *That wretched child is returning!*' the figure snapped, turning to one of the armed men.

'No!' the man pleaded. 'Please! I'll do anything!'

It was no use. In a bright white flash of light, he was turned into a TV.

The dragons fled to hide among the luggage, and the other armed man slowly backed away, trembling. They knew that no living thing could survive being swapped with objects from the Earth World.

The man in the glowing mirror grinned. 'That

boy – the Imposter – will be no match for you, once you have the power of this star glass, charged by the eclipse. We'll crush him. The Torch will be yours again. You are the true Ninth Dreamer! We can finish what you started.'

'I'll be on the ship by next sundown, Zamar, and in the desert with you in time for the eclipse.' Null laughed and the white mask slipped a little.

The armed man in the corner gasped.

The figure quickly straightened the mask, then raised an arm to the man.

He flinched. 'I didn't see anything!' he said. 'I swear! Please!'

With a flick of the figure's wrist, the train door opened to the bitter howling wind and the man was thrown screaming into the darkness.

Somewhere else in the same world, a sleeping boy in a travelling coach stirred.

In London, in the Earth World, Ben Thomson was having his recurring nightmare.

It always starts in a dark cave filled with shadows and screams. Ben can hear rasping breaths and the heavy footsteps of a monster. He can't see the monster, but he knows it's there.

Frantically, he searches for a way to escape – and then he sees it. A shaft of light up ahead. He hurries towards it; he can smell smoke and feel heat from behind, as if the monster is breathing fire. The footsteps lighten as it moves towards Ben, but he's almost at the light—

BANG! BANG! BANG!

Ben awoke to a violent hammering on his bedroom door.

'Really?' he groaned, pulling his thin duvet to his nose and glancing at his clock with dismay. The time was 5:09 a.m. Too early even for *his* alarm clock.

'I'm up!' he shouted, and the hammering ceased.

Then he heard a gentle nibbling sound by his pillow. He switched on his bedside lamp and turned his head to see a little brown mouse chewing the corner of a piece of paper.

'Oi,' whispered Ben, gently scooping up the mouse and placing it behind his bedside table, into a nest of torn-up paper. 'What if she sees you, Lucky?' he whispered. 'If she knew I'd rescued you from that trap . . .' He stroked Lucky's silky ears. Ben's affinity for animals was as strong as ever.

He sat up in bed, wearing his navy-blue coat for extra warmth, and took a few sunflower seeds from his pocket, which he'd pinched from next door's bird feeder. 'Have some actual breakfast,' he said. Then he smoothed out the piece of paper that Lucky had been chewing. 'It does look good, doesn't it?'

It was one of his own drawings. Ben loved designing buildings. He drew them on any scrap of paper he could find. This one was on the back of a coffee-stained shopping list. He had drawn an enormous department store, lavishly decorated for Christmas, its odd-shaped windows full of toys and books. On its wonky top floor there was a boy in a bright window, dunking gingerbread into hot chocolate.

'If only . . .' he sighed, seeing his breath in the frigid air. His dream was to be an architect one day and design real buildings. It was a dream he couldn't imagine coming true.

Then something odd happened to Ben. He felt a strange tingle in his hands and feet, like pins and needles. The clock's ticking seemed to be getting louder.

Ben tried to dismiss it. This had happened once before, on the magical day when he had blacked out and woken up in the Elf World, the world where his name was not Ben but Jayben instead. He had hoped to go back there. But that had been over a year ago. He was thirteen now and his hope of ever returning to his friends in that wondrous place was fading.

Ben had learnt that in order to switch worlds, he had to see his chord – the full moon. And so every full moon, Ben had stayed up past midnight to watch it through his window. But nothing had happened.

Last night had been a full moon, and Ben had stared at its big bright face until his eyes could stay open no longer. He was starting to feel desperate. His friends back in the Elf World needed him. He dreaded to think what might be happening in his year-long absence.

But again, nothing had happened.

Now he drew back his tatty grey curtains for one more look at the full moon before dawn, but the sky had clouded over and he was still here. Trapped.

BANG! BANG! BANG!

Again, that thumping on the door. 'Get up!' a woman's voice snapped from behind it. 'I know what you're like, you lazy so-and-so. I can't trust you when I'm not here. I'm not leaving until you've started cleaning.'

Samantha. Ben's aunt and guardian.

Ben had been living with her for the past seven years. He had only been six when he'd been brought here, though he had no memory of it. Samantha had told him his parents had died but wouldn't go into detail. He knew nothing of his life before – apart from one postcard his parents had sent him from a weekend away when he was little, and one precious memory of his mother, giggling with him in a phone box, and wishing him Happy Birthday.

This memory gave him hope that someday he would remember more of what must surely have been a happy childhood.

He knew he had suffered a brain injury seven years ago and that was the reason for his memory problems. But he still couldn't understand why Samantha resented him so much. One thing was for certain: ever since the day he had returned from the Elf World, life had gone from bad to worse.

Strange things had happened in the house that day.

Samantha's phone had turned into a warm chocolate gribblenut, one of his favourite things in Elf World.

Her boyfriend Marcus's car had been swapped for a horrible flying hemnik, a witch's pet, which had bitten Marcus before crumbling to ashes.

Ben remembered Samantha looking terrified as her phone was transformed at random. He, on the other hand, had found it exhilarating. He had no control over the power he had brought back from the Elf

World, but, having suffered his aunt's cruelty for so long, he couldn't help but smile to see her scared and bewildered.

To his crushing disappointment, the magic only lasted for a day. He knew better than to try and explain the Elf World to his aunt. Samantha had said many times before that anyone who believed in magic was a 'pitiful moron'. She insisted they must have been merely hallucinating, caused by exhaustion.

The trouble was that Ben had seen her vulnerable and afraid of the changing objects. And for that, he needed to be punished.

Samantha had searched his bedroom more thoroughly than ever, and uncovered the precious postcard from his parents, his only family keepsake. She found his drawings too. She took it all, and in its place she left him with extra homework. His alarm clock was set to wake him even earlier, so that he could do twice as many chores before school each day.

Ben had tried to push back – to question his aunt's behaviour. After all, he had defeated Null, a terrible villain in the Elf World, and saved his friends – surely he could stand up to Samantha? But for every protest, she would make his life even harder.

And there was no escape at school. She was also his form teacher at Milgrove Manor. Ben had accepted that the only way to survive was to obey.

Initially that hadn't been quite so hard. He had expected the first full moon to take him back to the Elf World. With every full moon that passed after he returned, to no avail, he began to consider the unthinkable. What if somehow he really had imagined the whole thing? What if he had never gone to the Elf World at all? He certainly had been exhausted that day . . . and it wasn't like his memory was reliable.

Ben's brain injury had been causing him to have seizures for a couple of years now. Sometimes in the school playground he'd find himself holding a ball but have no memory of catching it. He would start writing a sentence and then forget what he wanted to say.

He still had his drawing though. He drew furiously, hiding the sketches from Samantha, who saw them as an 'inexcusable waste of time'. But the designs wouldn't stop coming to him, designs he knew now were inspired by the Elf World. Houses with beams made of living plants, hotels with wavy-framed windows and skyscrapers with scaly, dragon-like roofs. Ben had always thought these ideas came from his imagination – until he visited the Elf World and discovered they were in fact all real. Though he couldn't quite remember the faces of his friends there – Phee, Peggro and Maybie – Ben could see the wonderful buildings clearly.

No. There was no way he had imagined the Elf World. Ben *knew* he had been there.

One good thing that had happened since his visit to that place was that Marcus, who had always been complicit in Samantha's mistreatment of Ben, had somehow softened. Since that strange day, when household objects had become magical, when Marcus's own car had transformed into a hemnik, Marcus had been quietly performing little acts of kindness for him whenever Samantha wasn't around.

Last Christmas, he had sneaked a funny comic book into Ben's bag.

On Ben's thirteenth birthday, he had slipped a chocolate bar into his lunchbox.

He'd even begun smuggling pens and paper into Ben's room.

One day, Marcus had discovered some of Ben's drawings. Ben had steeled himself for a fight. But Marcus had just stared at them. Then he'd said that

Ben had 'a remarkable gift' and promised that if they worked together, he could help him to achieve his dream of becoming an architect, and maybe even get away from his aunt.

'You've had it rough,' Marcus had said. 'Sorry I never stuck up for you sooner. It seemed easier just to go along with things. But I can see you've got talent, Ben.'

Part of Ben was reluctant to trust Marcus, after the way he had been treated. But Ben liked to believe in second chances, and he couldn't help but wonder whether the hemnik bite had somehow changed Marcus. Whatever the reason, he was glad to finally have some help. Who cared who it came from?

Ben yawned and stretched. Then he remembered what day it was. The twenty-fourth of December. Christmas Eve.

Rubbing his bleary eyes, he lifted the corner of his thin, lumpy mattress and retrieved a bright-red stocking, embroidered with a golden 'B' for Ben. He had found it in a dusty bin bag in the loft a few months ago while searching for his parents' postcard. Finding the stocking was fresh evidence of a happy childhood. Someone had loved him once.

He knelt up on his pillow to hang it on a rusty

nail sticking out of his dark-blue wall, between a long crack and a patch of mould. He wasn't expecting to find presents in it tomorrow. Last Christmas he had run downstairs to find two presents in the hall with his name on. But before he could unwrap them, they were snatched by his aunt. She explained with a smirk that until his grades improved he 'deserved nothing'. Until he was less 'hopeless'.

Deserved nothing. Hopeless. Ben forgot many things – but those words and the anger he had felt on hearing them wasn't going anywhere.

He paused, staring at the jolly stocking in his otherwise gloomy room, trying to imagine it hanging in a happy home again someday. Imagining it bulging with gifts. Sure, it was empty right now, but if something is empty then it can be filled, he liked to think.

'Get a move on!' Samantha called from downstairs. 'I'm not leaving until I know you're working. If you make me late . . .'

Lucky gave a little squeak.

'Shhhh!' said Ben, handing her another seed and quickly hiding his pens in his drawer. 'Down in a minute!' he shouted.

Ben glanced at the clock. It was 5:21 a.m.

He still hated clocks. They still made him late.

He looked at his drawing of the festive shop, grinning at the boy in the bright window. Maybe, with Marcus's help, that could be him one day.

He stuffed it into his pocket, carefully stashing the rest of his paper behind the bedside table to keep Lucky warm. Then he hopped out of bed fully dressed with a shiver, ruffled his short coppery hair and twisted the cold handle of his door.

As he did so, the clock's ticking grew louder. *Tick tick tick*. The tingles spread to his arms and legs.

It can't be the magic, he thought. The full moon had been and gone – yet again. *Could it be another seizure coming on?* He pushed the thought away.

There was one good thing about today. He was going to be alone. Marcus was taking Samantha to view some houses she was interested in buying. Ben was still puzzled how she could afford it. He certainly wasn't seeing any of her new money. But all that mattered to him right now was that Marcus had said they would be gone for hours. Being alone on Christmas Eve might not sound ideal – but for Ben it meant he could finally put on some music and doodle in peace. Nothing could stop him.

Almost nothing.

The Blizzard from the Bookcase

Ben plodded downstairs to find the front door open. In the dark outside he could see Samantha's tall frame standing by a frosty dustbin, holding a jug.

'Scram!' she hissed, flinging the water at a small fox with its head in the bin. It yelped and scurried away. 'Pathetic creature,' she said. 'Just because I've thrown it away doesn't make it yours!'

Ben stepped back as she returned, scraping her squeaky leather boots on the mat and slamming the door. Her black hair was already pinned for the day, and her sallow face already frowning as her piercing green eyes locked on to him.

'Happy Christmas Eve,' Ben muttered.

'Don't start with me,' she said, towering over him. 'Why is your top button undone? You'd better not have the heating on up there.'

'You know my room's always freezing,' he said. 'I slept in my coat.'

'Money doesn't grow on trees,' she said. 'It is earned. And it's not my fault that you're so completely hopeless.'

Hopeless. That word still hurt Ben. It stirred the burning anger inside. But, however unfair, he had to behave himself or risk losing what little freedom he had.

He tried to grit his chattering teeth.

Samantha looked at her watch. 'You forgot to set your alarm again, didn't you? Idiot.'

Ben wasn't sure. He just remembered staring at the full moon until late. 'I'm sorry, I didn't—'

'No excuses. Get started with your chores,' she interrupted, thrusting a mop and bucket at him.

Ben took a deep breath and dragged the mop out to the kitchen. He was hit by the peppery scent of a familiar aftershave, and found Marcus folding some paperwork into a blue binder labelled *Lipworth Lettings*. That was Marcus's company. He looked the same as always; tall, dark and handsome, if copious amounts of hair gel was your sort of thing. But now he had a scar on his hand, from the flying hemnik bite.

The kitchen clock read 5:27 a.m. Its ticking seemed louder than usual, even louder than the clock upstairs. *Tick tick tick*.

And now the dark windows were tapping with the first drops of rain. *Tap tap tap*.

Marcus glanced around to check they were alone, then grinned at Ben. He reached into his leather briefcase and handed him a large chocolate coin.

'Enjoy the peace today,' he whispered with a wink.

Ben's eyes lit up, but no sooner had the golden foil met his hand than it was swiped from behind.

'Nice try!' said Samantha. 'Using that tragic face to exploit Marcus. You don't fool *me*.'

'Oh, come on, Sams,' said Marcus, zipping his binder into his briefcase. 'It's Christmas Eve *and* we'll be gone all day.'

'Precisely!' she said, marching to the dining table. 'There'll be nobody here to make sure he's working. The way he's carried on this year, failing in every subject like it's all a big joke – he's done nothing to deserve any special treatment. Little brat cannot be trusted.' She unplugged the radio and stuffed it into one of her bags on the table.

Ben panicked. That was his music for the day. 'Please!' he begged. 'I'll be good. I'll clean the house much faster with the radio on.' Then he noticed the TV had been removed too.

'Rubbish!' Samantha said, slamming a pile of textbooks on the table. 'You'll be distracted and enjoy yourself while my back's turned. Now, get cleaning because I expect your homework to be done by the time I get back.'

Ben looked at the tall stack of work with dismay. He *needed* some respite. 'Please. I'll be better next term, I promise. If I have today off. Just one day.'

Samantha rolled her eyes. 'If it's not Christmas, it's a birthday, or a weekend, or a sick day – any excuse to be bone idle.' She went upstairs, shouting down to Marcus. 'You can start the car. I'm checking the heating is off.'

Ben swallowed. The clock's ticking grew louder still, and the rain fell heavier on the window. *Tick tick tick. Tap tap tap.*

The tingles spread to his arms and legs.

Marcus patted Ben on the shoulder and whispered, 'You have a gift, remember? She'll see it, one day. Just keep going and I'll handle it.'

The words helped but not enough. As much as Ben

appreciated the occasional smuggled treat and the promise of a brighter future someday, his life was miserable right now. Every day was agony.

'But how much longer?' he said. 'You don't know what it's like.'

'I know, mate,' Marcus said. 'Keep practising that talent of yours. You can do it. I'll bring some more paper tomorrow, all right?'

'I just wish I could get out of here.'

Marcus wandered out to the hall. 'Life's not a fairy tale,' he said.

Ben hated that line. He took the bucket to the sink with a heavy sigh, when something distracted him. A gentle white light shone from the window. It was the full moon, still up, fighting against the dawn, peeking through a narrow break in the cloud.

What do you want? He addressed it in his mind. *Stop teasing me. Go away, unless you're going to help get me back to Elf World.*

He watched it as rainwater started running down the glass. Through it, the moon appeared distorted, like it was dancing . . .

Like it was dancing . . .

Ben remembered. *The dancing moon!* It had appeared like this once before, on that fateful day

when he had been sent to the Elf World. He had forgotten – his chord wasn't simply a full moon. He needed to see the full moon *exactly as it looked in Elf World*. In Elf World, the moon always danced.

That's why it didn't work last night, or the other times, Ben thought excitedly.

He had seen it at last. His chord. The key to get him back to Elf World.

The tingling rushed to his head—

And the moon disappeared behind a cloud.

Tick tick tick. The kitchen clock hammered at his ears. He remembered something else. When his chord had appeared before, all of the clocks had stopped. Ben turned to the mantel clock in the sitting room and the new clock in the hall. They were all working.

He looked back to the window. The moon had gone and nothing had changed. But his whole body was tingling.

Was it the start of a seizure?

He sat down and held his head. He could hear Marcus starting his car outside and the groan of the dustcart rolling up the street. Every noise was too loud.

'What are you doing?' barked Samantha from behind him. 'Did I say you could take a break?'

'It's my head,' he said. 'I'm scared that I might be having a—'

'Oh, how very convenient,' she said. 'When I've just asked you to do something. I don't care what's wrong with you, you're not going to make me late for these viewings. Now, get on with it.'

Hot tears streamed down Ben's cheeks. He couldn't bear another Christmas like this. Without love. Without joy. Without kindness. All he had was hope, and he needed it now more than ever. But the dancing moon had been and gone without any effect on those greedy clocks.

Tick tick tick. Tap tap tap.

Was he really never going to return to his friends in the Elf World? Was he never going to get his power back? In Elf World, he had been Jayben. Magical. Possessor of the Golden Torch. He had fought Null. He had saved his friends.

Here, he was nothing.

The thought of it was crushing.

'I said, get on with it,' said Samantha.

Scratch scratch. Ben looked up. He saw the little fox outside, soaked and shivering. A look passed between them.

Ben flared his nostrils. His blood boiled with anger.

20

'No more,' he whispered.

Tick tick –

All the clocks stopped.

There was a bright white flash from the sitting room, like lightning.

Ben felt goosebumps all over, and Samantha shrieked.

Ben turned to see her pointing at a pile of red pine cones on the table, where the stack of textbooks had been.

'What did you do?' she cried. 'Where are the books?'

Ben stared at the pine cones, heart racing. He had Free-Dreamed. He had swapped something in the Earth World for something in the Elf World. Free-Dreaming required the most powerful magic.

He stood and peered at the pile more closely. Those pine cones looked like they were from the Memory Woods. Had the textbooks actually gone there? A sharp pain shot through his tingling head. He gripped the kitchen counter and let out a cry.

'Answer me!' Samantha barked.

Marcus returned, leaving his car running outside. Neither of them seemed to have noticed the clocks.

'Come on, Sam,' Marcus said. 'We're going to be late.'

'I don't know what happened,' said Ben. 'Please, just leave me alone.'

'Leave you alone?' Samantha gave him a cold stare. 'Not likely. How do you explain this?'

From behind her back she produced the precious red stocking from Ben's parents.

His stomach dropped. 'That's not yours!'

'You've got a nerve. Going through my loft so you can—'

'But it's mine!' said Ben, walking towards her. '*You* hid it from *me*.'

'You are a child; nothing belongs to you.'

Marcus jingled his car keys. 'We're going to be late.'

But Samantha wasn't done. 'Ungrateful brat,' she continued, passing the stocking to Marcus. 'You don't know how lucky you are. With your problems, you're lucky someone took you in. You'd be begging for hand-outs. So if I were you, I'd stop—'

'I don't need your help!' Ben snapped, shaking, his jaw clenched. 'When I'm an architect, I'll show you—'

Samantha broke into laughter. 'An architect? Don't make me laugh. You won't achieve anything in life. You are hopeless.'

That word again. *Hopeless.*

'Completely and utterly HOPELESS.'

'I'm not!' he cried, struggling to concentrate through the sharp pain in his head. 'I'm . . . I'm . . .'

He stopped.

Every noise in the house became even louder. Every light was too bright.

The storm was coming.

'Hopeless,' she said.

Suddenly he could hear the hasty tick of the mantel clock again. *Tick tick tick*. But it sounded sharper and deeper than usual. He looked up, breathing fast. The clock's hands were running *backwards*.

Then he heard the kitchen clock and the clock from the hall. All of the clocks. All of them ticking and tocking, from every corner of the house.

'For hell's sake!' Samantha shouted, grabbing him by the arm. 'What did you do now?'

BANG!

The mantel clock exploded. Everyone jumped.

BANG!

The clock in the hall shattered.

BANG!

The kitchen clock burst into flames.

The radio tumbled out of her bag and started screeching, like the squeal of a car's brakes.

Samantha backed into the corner, looking at Ben with that fear that he hadn't seen in over a year. 'Stop it! Now!' she cried, dropping her phone and handbag.

With another bright white flash, the phone turned into a glowing blue toadstool.

She screamed and ran for the door, but it slammed shut.

Ben looked at Marcus. A slow grin spread over Marcus's face. The hemnik bite on his hand was smoking slightly.

Samantha backed against the tall bookcase.

Pop! There was a flash behind her and one of the books became a pile of snow and a couple of pine cones.

She sprang back.

Pop! Another book turned to snow.

Pop! Pop! One by one, the books puffed into white powder, faster and faster.

Ben saw Samantha mouthing words at him but he couldn't make them out. Not over the tinny *screech* of the radio and the *tapping* of the rain and the wild *popping* from the books. *Pop pop pop.* He shut his eyes tight, trying to separate the sounds, but the noises were locking together, swirling around and attracting yet more sounds. Marcus's car growled outside, the dustcart bleeped incessantly, the men crashed the bins against it and next door's dog barked.

Ben cupped his hands over his ears, but he couldn't block out the noises. Then he smelled it. The room reeked, as if Marcus's aftershave was being cooked with rotten chicken. Now he could *taste* it. It was stinging the back of his throat.

He felt the air in the room moving and he opened his eyes to see the snow from the bookcase blowing into the air and swirling around the room as more and more books puffed into snow and ice. *Pop pop pop.*

The tingling sensation was like electricity buzzing around his body, and he could feel his heart beating hard.

Thud thud thud. Pop pop pop.

He shut his eyes and, like the first time he left this world, he saw the pink and yellow dots in his eyes, flashing like tiny fireworks, and, just when he felt as though he would burst, his arms thrashed out and he fell to the floor.

Down and down again, as if the ground had opened beneath him. Down he fell, until suddenly, with a loud crack, everything stopped.

Just as before, there was no sound and no smell

25

here, only stillness and darkness. His heart stopped racing, his breathing slowed. Every muscle in his body was still.

The blizzard from the bookcase had taken Ben's mind to the world far away.

CHAPTER 3

Hot Wheels Headed for the Ice

In the faraway world, a boy opened his eyes to see a lamp, swaying from a ceiling above him.

The boy had no memory. He felt calm at first. Everything was gently rocking. But then he remembered something: danger. He tried to move, but he was strapped down to a bed with leather belts, under a thick blanket. *Why was he tied up?*

Panicking, he tried to sit up, but he couldn't. He looked around to see dark curtains on all sides. *Where was he?* The place was quietly creaking and rocking from side to side. There was a fast, rhythmic crunching sound that seemed familiar, like hooves in snow. *How did he know that sound?*

Then came muffled voices from behind the curtain at his feet. His breathing quickened. He pushed his arms with all his strength and the belt across his chest snapped.

He sat up, feeling dizzy and sleepy. He was wearing a white shirt and he could feel something sharp in his trouser pocket. He reached in and pulled out a large yellow gemstone, the size of an orange. *What is this?* he thought, holding it to the lamp to see it glistening gold in the warm light.

Something shimmered in his palm too, flashing with different colours. A swirl of crystals embedded in his hand. Memories came flooding back. *The Rainbow! The crystals that give me my power!* He remembered then, with a rush of excitement, *I'm the Ninth Dreamer!*

The Ninth Dreamer. The last in a long line of Dreamers, and the one prophesied to stop Null destroying both worlds . . .

There was something in his other pocket, a circular object made of polished black wood with bold silver letters engraved on one side. It read:

JAYBEN

My name, he recalled. *And this is my compass. The one I found in my pocket, from Mum and Dad.*

He flipped it open to reveal the silver navigational dial and, engraved on the back, some words:

AS LONG AS YOU HAVE A HOME TO FIND YOU WILL NEVER BE LOST.

He knew where he was now. He could remember waking up and finding this compass, even if everything else was hazy. He was in the Elf World.

There was something else in his pocket – a large, almost transparent coin. The crystal shilling! He had been given it by Raynor, a Chordian Guard sent to protect him. She had told Jayben that he needed to keep the shilling close to absorb his powers or they would cause living nightmares for anyone around him. Gripping it tightly, he saw his reflection in the murky coin; short coppery hair, thin face. He looked slightly older than the last time he had been in Elf World.

He noticed a leather band on his wrist with a charm attached: a tiny, square blue nutshell. Memories came rushing back. It was his Trollwood charm on his clanband. He remembered that everybody here wore a charm, passed down the generations since the Magic Ages, to show which of the five woods their family was from. Jayben had discovered he belonged to the

Trollwood clan. He remembered his charm glowing, releasing his old family magic, when he had faced the evil, masked Null in battle – Null, who had wanted to take the Golden Torch from Jayben.

Closing his eyes. Jayben struggled to remember more. The Torch was not simply a magical object. It was one end of the magical pipeline through which the Energy must flow between Earth World and Elf World; the Energy we need for our memories to work. Though Energy was still flowing to Earth World, a giant's curse had stopped it flowing back to Elf World. The flame of Energy that had once burned night and day had gone out. And so, to keep their brains functioning, the people here were dependent on what little Energy could be absorbed by living close to the precious objects connected to Earth – the Free-Dreams. But it all depended on keeping the pipeline in place.

Instead of lighting the Torch, Jayben recalled, Null had wanted to break it, to close the Energy pipeline and plunge both worlds into darkness, erasing the memories of everyone in both worlds in the process, so they would believe what they were told and blindly follow Null's orders – total control. Jayben had reclaimed the Torch the day he had fought Null, and he had taken half of Null's Rainbow crystals, the crystals that gave Null his terrifying powers. The power to bring whatever he wanted from Earth World, including modern weapons. The power to move objects with his mind. And the power to spread curses, with the help of a witch accomplice. Null had been weakened but had escaped, leaving Jayben with the Torch—

Wait. The Torch! Where was it? He checked both pockets. It wasn't there.

Another memory came to him. Of the terrible moment just before he had fallen into a deep sleep, before he had crossed back to Earth World. The moment when he'd watched helplessly as his dear friend Tedrik had been put under Null's curse, turned into a nullhead, shuffling like a zombie into the night. To think that, like all nullheads, Tedrik would have no memories, left all but brain dead – it was unbearable.

'Tedrik!' he cried out.

A girl appeared from the curtain with a gasp. 'Ben! You're awake!' she squealed, eyes wide. 'Guys! Jayben's awake!'

Jayben took in her dark freckles, chocolate-brown eyes, brown hair in a ponytail and slightly pointed ears. He knew her! It was his friend Phee, about his age, wearing a thick red winter coat and scarf and her tiny red pine-cone charm on her clanband, the charm of the Giantwoods. She was Tedrik's daughter.

'Phee! Where's your dad?' asked Jayben, hopping up. He stumbled on the swaying floor, feeling even more dizzy. 'Where's the Torch? And why is everything here moving?'

'It's okay, Ben,' Phee said, helping him back on to the bed. 'Take it easy. It's been a whole year since you went to sleep. First things first. We're moving because we're in a carriage.'

The hooves pounded faster.

A whole year? Jayben couldn't imagine what might have happened in such a long absence. Once again he knew so little; he felt so unprepared.

'Why are we in a carriage?' he said, pulling the curtains behind the bed to find a small dark window, dusted with snow. 'Where are we going?'

'Oinff!' A green piggy snout appeared at the foot of the bed.

'Russog?' said Jayben, remembering Phee's pet skoggle.

'Oinff!' The creature leapt on to the bed. Russog had the body and paws of a dog, covered in thick,

green hair and brown spots, with three legs and a stump where his right front paw would have been. He remembered that a skoggle could imitate any voice they heard.

Jayben smiled, relieved in spite of his confusion to see his fuzzy little friend. 'I missed you, boy!'

The skoggle licked his face then lifted his curly tail, let out a loud fart and said in Phee's mother's warm, laughing voice, 'Charming!'

Jayben laughed but he couldn't shift the feeling of dread. He looked at Phee. 'Where is Tedrik? And where's the Torch?'

Before she could answer, the curtain was thrown wide open, letting in a gust of cold air and Jayben was delighted to see two more familiar faces in the carriage, looking just as excited as Phee.

'Peggro!' said Jayben, spotting his younger brother, who must now be ten.

Peggro's cheeks were still pale, his blond hair still neat and his glasses as well polished as ever. He wore his green egg charm around his neck, the charm of the Dragonwoods – the clan from their dad's side.

Jayben had discovered that Peggro and he were brothers in Elf World. Their dad had gone missing over a year ago, nullheaded, like Tedrik. He recalled with a pang of sadness their grandma, who he'd met last year, explaining that their mum had died when they were little.

He looked at Peggro's trusty brown leather satchel, still bursting with books and crumpled paper. It reminded Jayben of their first adventure together last year.

'Jayben!' said Peggro, with a grin from ear to ear.

Beside him was a girl with brown eyes and brown skin and a golden flower in her curly black hair, to match the golden nutshell charm around her neck. 'Jay-Jay!' She beamed, rushing to hug Jayben. As she flung her arms around his neck, he knew exactly who she was. It was their friend Maybie, from the realm of Fellooz – she must now be eight – wearing a fuchsia-pink fur coat.

'Oh, my wings!' she gasped. 'You're awake! And just in time!' Jayben noticed the tiny silver wings on her neck. She was of course a Fairywood, descended from the old fairies. With a sniff of the fairy dust in her charm, she could shrink down and fly.

Peggro's grin quickly turned to a look of concern to see the crystal shilling on the bed. 'Get that back in your pocket! It needs to stay right next to you to absorb your power, remember? Or the nightmares will happen again.' He shuddered. Then he noticed the large yellow gem. 'What in the world is that?' He peered closer. 'Jayben, that's star glass! It's from that tomb in Fellooz. It's super powerful. Where did you find it?'

Jayben shrugged, stashing the coin and his compass back in his pocket. 'I don't know. It was just in my pocket.'

Peggro took the yellow stone and frowned at Phee and Maybie, shaking his head. 'No, it wasn't *just in your pocket*,' he said. 'At least, it wasn't the other day. Last time we checked.'

The girls looked worried, which made Jayben even more nervous. 'Can one of you please tell me what's going on! And where is the Golden Torch?'

BANG!

There was the sudden sound of broken glass and they all jumped. Peggro dropped the gem. The window had been smashed.

'What was that?' cried Jayben.

BANG!

The carriage shook and the pounding hooves became erratic. In Maybie's voice Russog screamed, 'I wanna fly home!'

Jayben knew that banging sound, he realised – it was the sound of pellets being shot at them by Null's evil Agents, from their horrible flashpin weapons – one of many dangerous technologies Null had brought from the Earth World. Dreamers could Free-Dream, switch objects from one world to another – a dangerous practice and one that Null used for evil.

'Stay down!' said Phee, cradling Russog, who was shaking. 'Come to the front!' She crawled back through the curtains to a seat, and Peggro and Maybie followed.

Jayben hesitated. He could see the yellow gem where it had fallen, only inches away. *Star glass*, Peggro had called it. He figured there must be a reason why he had it – that it could be important. He scrambled forward to grab it, before shoving it back in his pocket.

'Come on, Jayben!' Phee called, and he crawled back towards the others.

BANG! BANG!

They heard a woman shouting from outside, in a voice that Jayben dimly recognised. 'Phee! I need you out here!'

Phee passed Russog to Maybie, pulled on a pair of leather gloves and whipped a handheld contraption from a bag. Jayben recognised it; it was similar to a crossbow – Phee's fishdart.

'Stay inside!' she said, clutching a pouch of arrows and tightening her scarf. She passed Jayben a blue winter coat, then turned a door handle next to the seat. The door flung open, blasting everyone with the icy night air. 'I'll be right back,' she said, gripping the doorframe and hoisting herself on to the roof of the carriage.

Peggro reached over and slammed the door shut, trembling. Maybie held Russog in the corner.

'No, Phee!' cried Jayben, horrified. 'Let me come with you.' He lunged for the door.

BANG!

Peggro grabbed his arm to pull him back. 'What are you doing? Phee can handle herself! It's *you* they're after! We need to keep you safe till we get there.'

'Get *where*?' Jayben asked, pulling his coat over his shoulders.

Peggro shook his head. 'We'll explain in a—'

Jayben wrenched away from him and opened the door, pulling himself out and up on to the snowy roof. 'Phee's out there on her own,' he called. 'And I'm going to help her – AAAH!' He struggled to grip the roof in the bitter wind. He could just make out that they were racing through the narrow backstreets of a dimly lit town.

'What are you doing?' shouted Phee from the front

of the carriage, aiming her fishdart to the rear. 'Get back inside!'

'I can't!' he said, crawling awkwardly towards her. 'I can't let them hurt you!'

Phee fired an arrow behind them, then ducked, pulling Jayben down to the driver's seat next to a young woman wearing a grey coat. She was gripping the reins, steering two black beasts . . . *trox*, Jayben remembered. Trox were like giant reindeer. They were panting wildly, shaking their antlers as they galloped at breakneck speed.

'Jayben!' cried the woman, taking a sharp left into an alley. In the light of a swinging lantern, he could see it was Raynor, the Chordian Guard who had helped him to fight Null and who'd given him the crystal shilling. 'You're actually awake!'

BANG!

Flashpin pellets pinged off the sides of the carriage and the lantern shattered.

Phee crouched on Raynor's left, brushing shards of glass off the seat with her coat sleeve.

'Keep low, Jayben!' Raynor shouted, tapping the trox with a long rod. 'Faster, girls! Faster!'

'What's going on?' shouted Jayben.

'It's Null's Agents,' Raynor explained. 'They'll do anything to stop us, now that they've finally found

you. Null needs you gone. You alone have the power to stop him, remember? The Final Dreamer. That's what the prophecy says. Unless Null gets to that tomb in time . . .'

'What tomb?' said Jayben, his head spinning, itching for information. 'How did Null find me? And why don't we have the Torch? It was in my pocket when I went to sleep. I thought it was safe.'

Phee stood up and shot another arrow before quickly ducking again.

'Hold on, Jayben!' said Raynor, as they galloped to the end of the alley.

'But I need to know,' he said.

'No, I mean literally hold on to something!'

Phee yanked on one of the reins and the trox took a hard right to avoid the blocked road ahead. The carriage leant, its left wheels leaving the cobbles for a moment.

'AAAH!' Jayben yelled, gripping the seat for dear life. They were thundering towards a tight gateway.

Raynor shouted back, 'Peggro! Maybie! Get down and cover your heads! Here goes . . .'

Jayben looked at the approaching arch. 'It's too low!' he yelled.

'Brace yourselves!'

Jayben and Phee ducked, covering their heads, as the trox shot through the gate.

SMASH!

The top of the arch ripped the roof of the carriage clean off.

'*FOR MOON'S SAKE!*' shouted Phee, as they cleared the gateway.

Peggro and Maybie screamed in the exposed compartment and Jayben could hear Russog too. 'Oinff! Oinff! Oinff!'

He carefully stood up, gripping the damaged top of the carriage to look inside. He could see the shady figures pursuing them, a dozen hooded cloaks riding grey trox as quick as the wind, and only a few yards behind.

'They're too close, Raynor!' He crouched back in the seat.

'Almost there!' said Raynor as they clattered through an empty street of shops, all closed for the night.

Almost where? Jayben wondered. Dazed, he watched the town flash by. As they sped past, Jayben read a sign in a shop window:

SECOND HAND SEA BOOTS
(may stink of fish)

Then he saw a banner across the street:

LAST ROCK HARBOUR
Turn right for standard cargo

We're near the sea, he thought.

Raynor steered them to the left.

Last Rock . . . Jayben had been here before. Last Rock was the capital city of the realm of Wenden, where he had lit the Golden Torch. They turned the corner and the vast city of snowy roofs and smoking chimneys came into view, sparkling in the moonlight and sprawling up a steep slope to the spectacular towers and turrets of the castle he had previously saved from an angry mob of Null's supporters.

Jayben looked back quickly to see one of the Agents was only a few feet away from the back of the carriage. 'They're gaining on us!' he shouted.

'It's okay,' said Phee, reloading her fishdart as they raced between brick warehouses and approached the tall masts of some enormous ships in the frozen dock. 'They must be running out of pellets by now—'

BOOM!

Flames exploded in front of them and the trox panicked, pulling in different directions.

'What the moon was that?' cried Phee.

Jayben looked back and saw one of Null's Agents holding a catapult and a glass bottle of liquid, stuffed with paper. There was a spark from the Agent's sleeve and the paper caught fire.

'Firebomb!' Jayben shouted.

He shielded his head with his arm as the lit bottle shot over their heads and smashed into a pile of crates on the dock, bursting into flames.

Raynor stayed focused, eyes fixed ahead. 'Here we are,' she breathed. 'Nearly there.'

Jayben squinted and in the darkness he could just about see the silhouette of a gigantic ship at the end of a very long pier.

BOOM!

A firebomb exploded at the entrance to the pier, ripping through the wooden structure and completely blocking their path.

Jayben looked left and right, his heart pounding. There were large groups of hooded figures on all sides.

'We're trapped!' shouted Phee, her fishdart shaking in her hand. 'That ship was our only way out!'

Trapped, with no escape. Jayben felt a sting of anger – he knew that feeling all too well. He looked beyond the waiting Agents, at the frozen sea in the bay and the tall ship in the distance. There was nothing but ice between them and the ship.

Ice . . .

'Hold on tight!' he said, putting one foot on the shaking harness of the carriage. Then he jumped on to the back of one of the running trox, grabbing its bridle.

'ARE YOU CRAZY?' shouted Raynor, trying to pull back on the reins.

Jayben yanked the trox's bridle to the right – *he had done this before, he knew that now* – and he steered both trox, aiming to the side of the burning pier, straight for the frozen sea.

'Jayben, NO!' shouted Phee, as the hooded Agents flung themselves out of the way.

Jayben leant forward and the trox's hooves leapt from the side of the dock, taking the carriage with them, its hot wheels headed for the ice.

CHAPTER 4

The Singing Shells

'AAAAH!' Jayben yelled as they landed awkwardly on the ice, hooves and wheels skidding. He forced himself to stay calm and urged the trox onward. 'Keep going!' he cried.

Obediently, the beasts continued, galloping alongside the pier, heading for the giant ship.

Raynor shouted back into the carriage. 'Peggro! Maybie! We're nearly there. Come up front!'

Jayben looked back to see Peggro and Maybie climbing nervously out of the carriage with Russog strapped into Phee's backpack.

'Here!' said Phee, helping Maybie into the seat next to her, before reaching up to help Peggro.

Jayben looked back at the docks. The Agents hadn't followed them on to the ice. Instead they were boarding the other ships and using firebombs to melt the surrounding sea.

The ice seemed to be getting thinner and thinner.

Crack!

The surface started to break behind the carriage.

'We're too heavy!' Raynor said. 'And the ice is melting. We'll never make it!'

Jayben looked ahead. They were nearing the ship and it now became clear how enormous it was, at least two hundred feet long with masts nearly as tall. There was a large crew gathered on its top deck and from one of the many open hatches in its hull, a rope ladder was being lowered to the ice.

Raynor was right, though – the carriage was too heavy. Maybe, Jayben thought desperately, if they were lighter they could make it . . .

'Everyone, get on the trox!' he yelled. 'We need to ditch the carriage!'

Crack!

Phee leapt over the harness on to the back of the other trox so that she was riding beside Jayben, helping Peggro and Maybie on behind her. Raynor jumped on behind Jayben, untying the harness from both trox, detaching the carriage and leaving it to sink behind them.

Crack!

The ice was failing in front and the trox slowed, uncertain.

Crack!

A large break in the ice formed ahead. The trox leapt over it, skidding uncontrollably.

'We need to finish this on foot!' cried Jayben. 'And let the trox get back to shore.' He leapt down and the others followed, all of them slipping and skidding towards the ship.

Jayben slammed into the wooden hull. They had made it! He reached out for the ladder, when—

Crack!

The ice broke from under him and Jayben plunged into the icy water. His body went cold and his muscles tightened. He thrashed about in a cloud of bubbles.

He saw something glinting in the darkness below. It was the crystal shilling from his pocket, sinking out of reach, vanishing into the deep. There was nothing he could do – it was beyond his reach.

Frantically, he kicked towards the surface. His legs began to stiffen as the cold and panic set in, when suddenly he felt hands on his arms. He was pulled back into the moonlight, gasping for air and shaking uncontrollably. His chest felt tight but he felt no pain. Of course he didn't; he was a Dreamer who only felt pain when switching back to the Earth World.

There were arms carrying him up the rope ladder – Raynor and Phee. Behind them were Peggro and Maybie. *Everyone has made it*, he thought.

Jayben put a hand into his pocket, hoping against hope that his compass hadn't fallen out along with the shilling – but he felt something hard and round. The compass! Relief flooded through him.

He felt the sharp gemstone too. *What is it – and why do I have it?* He wondered, as he was carried on to the ship, whether he would now get the answers to his questions.

Jayben couldn't hear much for the water in his ears, and it was dark, but in the moonlight he could make out the fuzzy outline of three tall ships full of Agents approaching, the vessels powered by giant propellers, their bows smashing through the weakened ice.

He was pulled backwards through the ship's hatch into a dark passage of flickering lamps. There were leaves sprouting from the ship's odd-shaped wooden beams, as thick as tree trunks. The leaves were twitching and he could hear a deep drumming noise from the wood, a beat he recognised. It was the same alarm the forest had sounded when he had first come to the Elf World, over a year ago, warning people of Jayben's powers and the living nightmares they could cause.

Without the crystal shilling, his magic was dangerous. He had to tell his friends – but his jaw was locked, chattering from the cold.

A few crew members hurried towards them, men and women wrapped in bulky clothes.

'Get him to the captain,' Raynor said to a man in a grey coat, taking a short spear from her belt, 'and get him warm. I'll be right there.'

Raynor ran off as shouts of 'Hands to propellers!' and 'Gunners to cannons!' could be heard.

The man in grey wrapped Jayben in a blanket, then slung him over his shoulder and slowly carried him through the ship. Jayben looked back and could see his friends following, passing a dozen hatches and a line of cannons. They were being loaded with something from barrels labelled:

SMOKED SAP
HIGHLY ADHESIVE

BOOM!

One of the cannons was fired, and through another hatch Jayben could just see one of the Agents' ships being showered with what looked like orange slime. Strings of it wrapped around the blades of the propellers, jamming them and bringing the Agents' ship to a halt.

Jayben's ears were ringing from the explosion, but he could hear chains dragging against the deck as he was carried into another section of the ship, where men, women and children were walking in a circle around a central pole, pushing against long handles to twist it. A mechanism of cogs labelled *Propellers* sprang to life and suddenly everything tipped to the left. Then it tipped to the right. Then left again.

'It's okay, Ben,' said Phee. 'We're moving now!'

'Oh, good,' he heard Peggro groan, before retching as the ship jerked forward.

Jayben could hear something else. *Singing.*

Deep voices bellowed from all sides. He squinted in the dim light to see large grey shells stuck to the beams of the ship. They were moving! The two halves of each shell opened like a mouth, singing in harmony.

'I'm gonna be sick!' cried Peggro.

The singing shells upped the tempo and the crew

turned the pole faster, as Jayben was carried up a dark crooked staircase with sloping walls.

He could still hear chains, rattling as they climbed to a little door. The man knocked, then opened the door and carried Jayben into pitch blackness.

'Oinff! Oinff!' said Russog from Phee's backpack as the beams of the ship drummed louder and faster. In Tedrik's deep voice he said, 'Stay here, boy.'

Phee, Peggro and Maybie followed inside.

'Wha-wha-what is this ship?' asked Jayben, finally gaining some control of his chattering jaw. 'Whe-whe-where are we going?'

Somebody struck a match in the darkness to light a lamp. Jayben could see an old woman with creased, tanned skin, holding the lamp, not with a hand but with a hook. A faded red eyepatch covered one eye. 'That'll be all,' she said. Her voice was a rough squawk.

The man put Jayben down next to a bucket and walked back to the door. Jayben realised the clanking sound was coming from the man, who was dragging a chain behind him.

As the man closed the door, Jayben saw a logo stitched on his sleeve. His heart skipped a beat.

Nine white squares, and the words: *Agents of the Ninth*.

CHAPTER 5

Death Can't Help You Now

Jayben's heart pounded. 'AGENT!' he cried, scrambling backwards.

Phee drew her fishdart from her belt, aiming it at the woman. 'This is meant to be a safe ship! Where's the captain?' she snapped. 'What have you done with him?'

'Captain?' the woman chuckled, lighting another lamp. 'You're lookin' right at her, kid!'

Phee looked surprised and half lowered her dart. '*You're* Captain Winnibar?'

The old woman nodded, using her hook to adjust her eyepatch. 'All the parts of me those pesky dragons couldn't stomach.'

Dragons? Had this woman really survived a dragon attack? She was very short, even shorter when she removed her purple hat with turquoise feathers, to reveal a mop of silver curls. There was a gold nutshell charm around her neck, like Maybie's, the charm of the Fairywoods, and she wore a garish orange jacket with a pink trim and gold buttons, electric-blue trousers and a lime-green boot on one leg. The other had been replaced with a wooden peg.

'But that man was an Agent?' asked Jayben.

Peggro grabbed the bucket and vomited. 'Someone throw him overboard!' he gasped, before heaving again.

'BAH!' the captain laughed. 'Why give him the satisfaction? No. When a man boards my ship without permission, he will leave on *my* terms. Why do you think he wears those chains?'

The ship groaned and drummed louder. Captain Winnibar took a sword from her hip and used it to prod one of the beams. 'You cut that out! Right now! Or I'll take us north again. Ya hear?'

The leaves shrank and the drumming stopped.

She shook her head. 'Odd. They haven't done that in a while.'

'It's a warning,' Jayben said, looking up at his

friends. 'I'm so sorry, guys. I lost the shilling! It slipped out when I fell through the ice. I couldn't reach it. I still have these, though.' He took out his precious compass and the large yellow gem.

Captain Winnibar approached. 'What a beauty!'

'Yes,' said Phee, 'but I'm still trying to work out how it got into your pocket, and why?'

'Magic?' Maybie suggested, wide-eyed.

Peggro, though, had turned even paler. 'You lost the shilling?'

Phee put her arm around Jayben. 'We'll get a new one. Don't worry.'

'*Don't worry?*' said Jayben. 'Don't you remember last time? All the horrible stuff that happened because of me? The fires? The storms? The dangerous animals drawn to us?' He turned back to the captain. 'I can't be near your crew. It's not safe for them. Things will happen. They could even die!'

To his surprise the captain laughed. 'Die?' she howled, with a twinkle in her eye. 'They should be so lucky! You're on the *Beth Rose* now, dear boy, where nobody gets off that easy. Death can't help you now.'

Jayben found himself returning her smile. He couldn't help but like Captain Winnibar, this tiny old woman who was commanding an enormous ship and crew, surviving dragon attacks, capturing Agents, even laughing at the mention of death, not to mention unapologetically wearing every single colour all at once. She seemed to embody all the courage and confidence that he needed right now.

'But what about the light, Jayben?' asked Peggro, still crouched over his bucket. He turned to the captain to explain. 'Jayben has a special light – a chordian light – that the Agents can see with their purple lenses. Without the coin to absorb his power, the Agents will see his light from miles away.'

Jayben hadn't had time to consider the light. It meant they were a beacon for the Agents – because of him. His stomach twisted.

'Snap out of it, kids!' said Captain Winnibar, untying a sack that was bulging with reels of gold ribbon. Cannons blasted in the background. 'I'm not worried about that light. Them old Chordian Guards have paid your fee in full, so we're hot to trot. We'll get ya there, dear Dreamer.'

'Get me where?' asked Jayben.

Peggro retched, hunched over the bucket.

'Now, what can we do about you?' said Winnibar. She reached up to a shelf and fetched a jar full of squirming blue worms. She took two out and gave them to Peggro, who dropped them immediately, grabbing the bucket again.

The captain laughed, picked the worms up and placed them on his wrists. The worms coiled tightly. Peggro looked baffled. But he stopped retching and the colour returned to his cheeks.

Captain Winnibar gave him a wink. 'You can never have too many burble worms on a boat full of kids.'

Peggro smiled. 'Thank you!'

There was a knock at the door and a boy about Jayben's height came in, carrying a neatly folded pile of dry clothes. 'Here you go, Granny,' he said, handing them to her. He glanced at Jayben. 'Will he be okay?'

'He'll be fine. Thank you. Now, back to your wheel, dear.'

The boy grinned and scurried out.

Jayben was intrigued. 'You have your grandchildren on this ship?'

Winnibar nodded. 'All thirty-three of the little rascals. Growing up like bad seaweed! Come on, let's get you out of those wet clothes.'

She showed Jayben to a closet where he changed out of his soaking clothes and into a fresh white shirt and some brown trousers, making sure his compass and the gemstone were safely in the pockets.

'Come on,' called the captain. 'We haven't got all night.'

He re-joined the others and they followed the captain through another door, into a vast cabin packed full of old books, reaching up to its high ceiling. It was a library! The wonky bookshelves were gently lit by hundreds of tiny white lights; some were attached to the books' spines.

Peggro yelped. One of the lights had found its way on to his satchel and was trying to get inside.

Jayben looked closely. It was a kind of glowing beetle with an oval shell.

'Bookles!' exclaimed Maybie, admiring one on a shelf. 'How adorable! I've never seen so many. We have some in school back home, but nothing like this!'

'How have I not heard of these before?' asked Peggro, taking out his notebook to find the shining bookle attached to it.

Captain Winnibar chuckled. 'Little nippers can't resist a new book. Now, sit down all of you and get warm.'

She handed Jayben a fresh blanket that had been warming by a stove at the centre of the rocking,

creaking library. Everyone sat on a thick rug in front of the stove and Captain Winnibar lifted a large can off it.

'This'll get you back in business,' she said, and she took a thick waffle cone from a wooden box and scooped it into the hot can. With the steam came a deliciously sweet aroma.

'Cropple cones?' drooled Phee, her eyes as big as saucers. 'Now you're talking!'

Jayben's mouth watered as Captain Winnibar handed him the cone, filled with a generous scoop of some sort of creamy dessert. The cone was delightfully warm in his hands. 'Oh!' he said as his tongue met the most heavenly mixture of buttery biscuit crumbs, caramel cream and big chunks of a juicy fruit that tasted just like apple. 'This is the best thing ever!' he declared, taking a massive chomp.

Maybie devoured hers. 'Where have these been all my life?'

'Not bad, are they?' said Captain Winnibar, snapping off a piece of cone for Russog, who let off a fart.

'Away from the stove, Stinkbomb!' said Phee.

Jayben never wanted to leave this enchanting library and he wondered how many more weird bugs and tasty treats they'd find aboard the *Beth Rose*. But unfortunately, there were more important, more urgent things that he needed to know.

'Could someone please tell me what's been going on for the last year?' he asked, as they were crunching the last of their cones. 'Where is Tedrik? Where's the Golden Torch? And where are we going?'

'Sorry, Ben,' said Phee. 'It's been a long time. First of all, Dad disappeared the night you went to sleep. He went out and never came back. We've searched everywhere we can think of, but nobody has seen him, so—' She broke off, biting her lip.

'No, *I'm* sorry,' Jayben said, shuffling closer. 'I – I saw it.'

Phee drew in a sharp breath.

'I remember sitting by the window,' he continued, 'when I saw a nullhead whisper to your dad and lead him away.' The whispers from a nullhead would transform a person, wipe all their memories and thoughts, before they had a chance to fight back, turning the person into a nullhead themselves. 'I tried everything to tell you – to scream – but I couldn't move, because I was going to sleep, back to the Earth World.'

Phee let out a sob.

'We assumed the worst,' she whispered. 'It's not your fault, Jayben.'

'So Tedrik *was* nullheaded,' said Peggro. 'Like our dad, Jayben. I knew it.'

Jayben recalled the bittersweet moment when he had found his grandma, living not far from Phee's house in the Giantwood, who had revealed that Jayben and Peggro were brothers. She'd also told them that their mother had sadly died when they were little, in an accident on a frozen lake.

Peggro had been too young to remember he had a brother – their doctor father took Peggro with him to the realm of Bramalan to treat others, when Jayben was in his deep sleep, in the care of their grandma. Years later, when Jayben woke up, he had wandered out into the woods, confused, and that's where he'd met Phee's family, Maybie and Peggro, who had lost their nullheaded father. He was still missing. Then he'd learnt that they had a grandpa called Mandon, who had gone looking for Jayben and never returned. The reunion with their grandma had been joyful and heartbreaking all at once.

'Like my pappa, too,' said Maybie, stroking Russog. 'He was nullheaded when I was six. It's so horrible.'

Captain Winnibar tutted, shaking her head. 'The

suffering that wicked Null has inflicted on so many families, so he can exploit their fear and enslave their nullheaded loved ones. But you can stop him, dear boy.' She looked at Jayben. 'Everyone heard what you did at that no-good bridge of Null's. Drove him away – and that terrible witch of his. Spectacular!' She raised her cone, as if making a toast.

'Null got away, though,' said Jayben, worried.

'With half of his powers gone, I heard.' The captain winked.

During the battle, Jayben had somehow summoned his ancestral Trollwood power, allowing him to move anything made of metal or rock with his mind, to take the Torch back from Null, who'd stolen it from Jayben.

'He's been lying low ever since,' said the captain, with great satisfaction. 'You defeated him once; you can defeat him again. For good.'

'But I had the Torch last time,' Jayben said. 'It was in my pocket when I went to sleep. What happened to it?'

Peggro looked sheepish. 'We still don't know. We thought you were safe in your room, asleep. We checked on you loads. The Torch was always in your pocket – until we checked again at the start of winter. We realised it was gone. We're not sure exactly when

it was taken – or how someone could have got in to steal it. Raynor alerted her fellow Chordian Guards immediately and they started searching all of Wenden.' He hesitated. 'Do you remember the Jarmaster?'

Jayben nodded. Every village in every wood had a Jarmaster, who stored people's memories in jars strung on the local helicorn tree and kept them safe. The Jarmaster in Phee's village, where Jayben went after he woke up, was a kindly old wise man living in the treehouse at the heart of the village.

'Well, he got some news on his network. He heard that the Torch had been seen in Fellooz a few days ago – on its way to Zamar!'

Captain Winnibar waved her hook. 'Zamar? That pompous fool?'

Jayben was more puzzled the more he heard. 'Who is Zamar? Why would he want the Torch?'

'Zamar is Null's ally in the realm of Fellooz,' said Peggro gloomily.

Maybie crossed her arms. 'And a very bad man,' she said. 'With lots of other baddie men helping him. Null sent him to Fellooz a few years ago to bring it under his control. He came to my hometown, Karassan, with his band of thugs. They rounded up all the Fairywood kids who couldn't escape. They took their wings! That's why we had to leave our home – my mum and my sisters and cousins. We made it out.' She shivered. 'That's when my poor pappa got nullheaded, and my aunt.'

Jayben stared in horror. 'I'm so sorry, Maybie. That's evil.'

Peggro nodded. 'Well, he is Null's ally. What would you expect? Zamar somehow got hold of the Torch and he has it in Fellooz. Raynor's spies say Null was seen journeying in that direction. It's clear he means to give Null the Torch.'

'So is that where we're going now? To Fellooz?' Jayben interrupted. 'Null can't control the Torch, because I took half of his Rainbow crystals, didn't I? I remember Raynor saying that I'd weakened him. Now he doesn't have enough power to control the Torch. Right?'

Phee nodded, but she looked worried. 'Not yet. But we think we know why Null is going to Fellooz. The solar eclipse.'

'What are you talking about?' Jayben said. 'A solar what?'

'A solar eclipse,' said Peggro, looking only too pleased to explain. 'It's when the moon gets in the way of the sun. It blocks out the light.'

'Goes really dark in the middle of the day!' said Maybie, with great enthusiasm. 'Gan-Gan told me! She was my age when the last one happened, nearly a hundred years ago!'

Jayben couldn't imagine it. 'Dark at midday? Sounds cool. But what does that have to do with anything?'

Phee pointed to the Rainbow crystals in Jayben's hand, the swirl of darker crystals in the middle twinkling in the light of the stove. 'You're right – with only half of his crystals, Null isn't powerful enough to control the Torch. But the solar eclipse in Fellooz could change that.'

The beams of the ship gave an ominous groan and Russog burrowed into Phee's lap, burping nervously.

'What do you mean?' asked Jayben uneasily.

Captain Winnibar picked up Jayben's yellow gemstone and spoke softly. 'There's an ancient tomb in Fellooz, in the scorching desert. It's full of yellow star glass gems, just like this one. The Chordian Guard say that when the moon blocks out the sun, it leaves a ring of magical light in the sky. If shone through a star glass gem, it can super-charge any crystal.'

She handed the gem back to him and continued. 'Hasn't been a total eclipse for a long old time so folk are excited to see it. Little do they know what a gift it'll be for that wicked Dreamer, if he can get to the tomb of star glass on time. Under that magical ring of light, he need only touch one of these yellow gems to his Rainbow crystals and he'll be three times more powerful. We think that's exactly what he intends to do.'

'Yes,' said Peggro quietly. 'Raynor's spies say that Null is only a few days away from Fellooz. If he gets there, to that tomb, for the eclipse, he'll be stronger than you again. More powerful than ever.'

'And Zamar has the Torch waiting for him too,' said Jayben, a sick, scared feeling in his stomach.

'That's right,' said Phee. 'Once Null has the Torch *and* the power to control it, he can finish what he started. He can use it to close the pipeline between the Earth and Elf Worlds for ever. He can take all the worlds' Energy, to wipe all our memories and control everyone.'

'We can't let that happen!' said Jayben.

'We won't,' said Phee, her expression determined. 'You're powerful, Jayben. You're the Ninth Dreamer!'

Jayben groaned. 'I still can't control my powers, remember? Last year I was struggling to Free-Dream objects from the Earth World.'

'Well, you managed it on the bridge!' cried Peggro. 'You threw a car and a big red bus at Null! Knocked him clean off!'

'But I didn't mean to,' said Jayben. 'Memories of those things came to me at random. I didn't choose to remember them and bring them here from Earth.'

Maybie shook her head. 'The Chordian Guard said that when you saw the almost-full moon that night, on our way to stop Null the first time, it must have been enough to unlock the power of your Rainbow crystals. You should have your full powers now – you just need to learn to control them.' She smiled. 'Maybe you just need to practise Free-Dreaming, Jay-Jay?'

Phee nodded. 'Maybie's right. Your powers are in you, Ben. Once you've figured it out, you'll be able to Free-Dream any object you want.'

For a moment, Jayben felt a flicker of hope. But he couldn't help but worry about the danger his magic would bring until he could control it. On their last adventure, they had been stalked by their own nightmares, summoned by Jayben's wild powers. Without the crystal shilling to absorb it, he knew it would bring people's worst fears to life again.

The ship groaned.

Winnibar stood up and used her hook to draw a

curtain between two bookshelves, exposing a frosty window. 'You're the famous Ninth Dreamer,' she said, watching the lights of the city of Last Rock disappearing on the horizon. 'That's why you're on my ship, dear boy. Have no fear. We'll get you to Fellooz by sundown tomorrow. Then you can journey to that tomb and guard it from Null.'

Maybie pulled a map of the Elf World from her pocket and pointed to the realm of Fellooz. 'Raynor says more Guards will meet us on the shore, not far from Karassan. They'll take us across the desert to the tomb, just outside Zamar.'

'I thought Zamar was a person,' said Jayben, bewildered.

Winnibar rolled her eye. 'A person *and* a city. Can you believe that meathead Zamar actually built a city in the desert, just so he could name it after himself? Talk about insecurity!'

Phee smirked.

'And to think that the great realm of Fellooz is now ruled by that grotesque bully,' the captain continued, 'since Null sent him there. Outrageous!'

Phee pointed to Fellooz on the map, where pictures of fairies were moving about. 'Raynor says it'll take a day and a night to cross the desert.'

'We'll make it in time!' said Maybie.

The ship began drumming again and the shells below deck sang louder. A warning – a warning that Jayben was here, just like last year in the woods.

Jayben shuddered. What kind of terror would his power conjure this time? He pushed the thought away – he needed to focus. 'Okay,' he said, tracing his finger across the map from Last Rock, over the sea to the coast of Fellooz and its Fairywood forest, then across the desert to Zamar's city. 'So we could be at that tomb near Zamar . . . in three days?'

'*If* all goes to plan,' said Peggro. 'Raynor's spies in the realm of Bramalan said Null's train was spotted on its way there a few days ago. He could be at sea by now too – ahead of us!' He looked unsettled by all the noise.

Jayben knew what the living ship was afraid of. Him.

The wood drummed faster and the shells sang louder still.

Captain Winnibar smacked her hook against the ship. 'Pipe down!' she squawked.

Jayben tried to ignore the warning. 'When is this solar eclipse supposed to happen?'

'On Day 6 : 360,' said Winnibar. 'Four days from now. At noon.'

Four days? And they would reach Fellooz in three. If they were lucky. But if anything went wrong . . .

The drumming became erratic and the shells were almost shouting. The deck shook at Jayben's feet and books began tumbling off the quivering shelves. His heart raced as he remembered his arrival in the Giantwood forest, over a year ago. He heard Tedrik's deep voice in his mind. *When a tree tells you to run, Jayben – you run.*

But now they were at sea. Now there was nowhere to run from danger – and no turning back.

CHAPTER 6

The Only Book No Bookle Will Touch

Jayben glanced at his friends, who looked as worried as he felt. Last time, his powers had conjured their worst fears – he couldn't put them through that again.

'You guys need to stay away from me,' he said. 'Somewhere else on the ship, until we get to Fellooz.'

'We're not leaving you alone,' said Peggro, clinging to his satchel. 'You're not safe either.'

Maybie took Jayben's hand. 'You only just woke up, Jay-Jay. We missed you.'

Captain Winnibar kicked the ship with her wooden leg. 'Final warning!' she snapped, 'Quit that racket or I'll give you something to drum about!'

The ship softened the alarm once again and the singing shells hushed down.

'We're not going anywhere, Ben,' said Phee, putting the books neatly back on their shelves. 'We survived last time because we stuck together, remember?'

Jayben paused and cast his mind back, but his memories were still murky. 'I *don't* remember,' he said, feeling totally overwhelmed, holding his head. 'Not completely, at least. It's like I'm remembering flashes here and there – but most of it doesn't make sense.'

'Of course not,' said Peggro, coming to his side. 'I mean, you've been asleep for over a year! And you were pretty forgetful before that too. We can help, though. We've figured out a way to show you everything—'

Phee shook her head at Peggro. 'Peggro, not now. Ben needs a rest. It's too much all at once.'

Peggro shrugged. 'But Jayben hates not knowing, don't you? And you always forget stuff, after your seizures.'

Jayben felt a chill down his spine. *Seizures?* The word brought painful memories of being confused, frustrated, injured and afraid. His cheeks felt hot and his eyes welled with tears. They were both right: it

was too much and yet he always preferred to know.

'I think,' he said quietly, 'that I would like to know what happened, if you can help me.'

Phee put her arm around him and took a small parcel out from her backpack.

'I remember this,' said Jayben. 'You gave this to me at Miraclest, as I was falling asleep.'

She grinned at him. 'That's right. Now you can open it.'

He carefully tore the wrapping to reveal a blue journal with a title:

Jayben's Remindary

He opened it and found every page full of handwritten notes and stories. Some entries were neat; others were written in big, messy letters.

'We all helped,' said Maybie, pointing at a scribbled picture of Jayben, Phee, Russog, Peggro and herself standing by a waterfall, where a fierce grannix, like a silver bear with antlers, roared at them. The drawing stirred a dim memory in Jayben's mind – of meeting the terrifying creature's eyes and connecting with it. 'We wrote down everything that happened to us together,' she said, 'just in case you forgot.'

Jayben turned the pages. He didn't know what to say. It was amazing. His friends were amazing. It was all there, every day of his adventure – since he'd first woken up on Day 8 : 99 (eight years and ninety-nine days until the next Big Miracle, whatever that might be). He remembered that in Elf World the calendar counted not up but down, to a miracle, every hundred years. Day 8 : 99 was the day he had met Tedrik, Russog, Phee and her mother Larnie in the Giantwood.

Every day was lovingly chronicled, right down to Day 8 : 01 (Miraclest Eve) when he'd gone back to sleep – and gone back to Earth World. With every drawing and story his memories sharpened. He read some of them aloud:

Day 8 : 98
Maybie: After you saved us from that big furry grannix, I shrank down so I could fly home but then we were chased through the woods by a lady we thought was an Agent, but of course later we found out it was actually just Raynor, trying to help us (oops!) Then there was a horrible darkning storm. And then we left the forest . . .

Day 8 : 97

Peggro: A witch called Snaggis, from the North (a Spritewood), who was helping Null, attacked us with her horrible flying pet hemniks. You lit the Golden Torch and drove her away. Then you Free-Dreamed something for the first time – a strange red postbox . . .

Day 8 : 96

Maybie: Before we could get on the boat in Blanbor, your poor head had a big bad seizure and you needed a good long rest, all day and night.

Day 8 : 95

Phee: At Last Rock Castle you lit the Torch, freeing any Nullheads who could see it from Null's curse! BOOM! It stopped his Agents and the angry mob from invading the castle. We wanted to get you to the Chordian Guard for help, but we were betrayed and taken to Null's bridge . . .

As he read, Jayben could slowly feel fragments returning. He remembered the battle on the bridge, his fear and exhaustion as Null had tried everything to kill him and break the Torch – to close the pipeline. He read the entry from Peggro:

Null had seized the Torch. He used his powers to throw Earthly objects at us, driving us on to the broken bridge. The battle raged, and Null and that witch seemed unstoppable. They began closing the pipeline, draining all Energy from both worlds and removing your Rainbow crystals which would have killed you . . .

But when all seemed lost, something amazing happened.

A memory came to you from Earth World – of a big red bus. You brought it here, trapping Null behind it. Then suddenly you gained your old magic, the magic from our Trollwood ancestors . . .

'My charm?' said Jayben, looking down at the blue, squared-shaped nutshell on his wrist. 'I remember it glowing . . .'

'Yes,' said Phee, showing her own charm, a red pine cone on her wrist. 'On the bridge with Null your powers were wild, almost uncontrolled. You were Free-Dreaming objects. Your powers even drew the ancient magic from *our* blood, from our ancestors in the Magic Ages. Maybie could suddenly heal wounds, like the old fairies could. I became ridiculously strong like the giants I'm descended from. And Peggro could turn invisible, just like the dragon folk in the past.'

Jayben stared at her, eyes wide. He could remember it – that intoxicating rush of power.

'But it didn't last long,' Phee went on. 'Once Raynor gave you the crystal shilling, to absorb your power, all our charms stopped glowing. It was safer that way, she said. Your powers could help save us – but until you can learn to control them, they'll bring us danger too. Then you went to sleep for ages, and we haven't had any magic powers since.'

Every answer brought another question to Jayben's mind. 'Why do we have different charms?' he asked.

'There are five different charms,' she explained, 'worn by every elf, on our clanbands, They show which of the five Memory Woods our families lived in, back in the Magic Ages, when the Torch burned, day and night, before that wicked giant put the curse on it. When he put the Torch out, the Energy drained away and gradually our ancestors forgot their magic. But the magic's still in our blood. If it wasn't for the Energy from the Free-Dreams we'd have no memories at all. Good job they can still draw some Energy from the pipeline, unless it breaks . . .'

Jayben closed his eyes, remembering the clans, one for each of the five Memory Woods of Elf World – Giantwood, Fairywood, Trollwood, Dragonwood and Spritewood. Null had worn a Trollwood charm. Null was of the same clan as Jayben – both were able to move rocks and metal with their minds.

'Here,' said Maybie, taking out her map. 'Let me show you the five realms.'

Jayben looked. It was, of course, no ordinary map; it *moved*. The seas sparkled between the five realms, and the trees of the five Memory Woods rustled. And there was Fellooz, home to the Fairywood. It was mostly desert. Jayben could see something like a giant green spider shifting behind some cacti, as a sandstorm rolled by. Further into the desert he noticed a few tombs dotted about. One was twinkling with yellow gems.

At the bottom of the map there was a bold, grey line, labelled *The Equator*, and below it, the tip of a dark forest of mysterious moving shadows. In tiny print, it simply read:

The North

Spritewood

(Don't Go here)

'I remember something about the fifth realm,' Jayben said slowly. 'It's dangerous, but no one knows why. There's sorcery there – not old magic, but dark magic, used by corrupt witches and wizards.' He turned to the captain. 'Have you got a copy of *The Book of Dreamers* here?'

The Book of Dreamers was a history of the eight famous Dreamers before Jayben. Eight girls and boys who could Free-Dream objects between Earth World and Elf World. Jayben was the Ninth and Final Dreamer.

Captain Winnibar pointed her hook to a dark corner of the library. The glowing bugs seemed to be avoiding it. 'You're welcome to read my copy; the only book no bookle will touch.'

Jayben was intrigued. 'Why not?'

'Those missing pages,' she said, and Jayben remembered that several chapters of the famous book had a blank page, where a page had been torn out of the original. Including the chapter about him. 'Something about those blank pages bothers 'em,' she said.

'I know the feeling,' Jayben said, going to fetch it.

The ship tipped and he gripped the bookshelf, pulling himself to a green armchair.

The others followed and gathered round as Jayben inspected the red leather-bound book with a title embossed in gold.

The Book Of
Dreamers

by
The Scholars Of Formadon

He recognised the gold symbol below the title: a pipe-like object with a swirl at one end. 'The Golden Torch,' he said, opening the book to Chapter One:

The First Dreamer

'So the Torch is not just a Torch. It's a pipeline from this world to the Earth World, and the Energy flows through it. And the Torch I carried is one end of it. And both worlds need the Energy, right?'

Phee nodded.

'It's a powerful memory force. It's what allows our brains in the Earth World and here in the Elf World

to access memory. Without it, people in either world will forget who they are and struggle to think or form ideas. I remember your mum telling me all this. Without the Energy, people become gullible and vulnerable and easily exploited. And the Energy has to flow equally both ways.'

He pointed to an old illustration of two parallel worlds, carefully drawn in pen and ink; two spheres joined by a long object.

One sphere was labelled *Earth World*, the other *Elf World*. The slender stream connecting them was labelled *The Golden Torch*.

'Earth needs Energy from Elf World, and the Elf World needs it from Earth. And they've always been connected. Our Energies must work together. That's what Null wants to stop. So that he can rule two worlds of people without thoughts or ideas and bend them entirely to his will.'

Jayben shivered. He turned to page one hundred and forty-two, the final chapter. 'This is my bit.'

The Ninth Dreamer

Evil shall threaten the elves once more. A dark force will rise and plot to wipe every mind in the world.

79

*When all seems lost, **One Final Dreamer** shall appear with the Blue Moon, when the Southern Lights are aligned.*

On Earth a child shall see a chord, and his mind will be taken far away, to the brain of his elfling self, in the Elf World.

He shall awaken a powerful Dreamer, with the Rainbow held in his hand. He shall find the Golden Torch, and harness his power to Free-Dream.

He alone must save every elf's mind from being wiped.

The Ninth Dreamer shall be the final Dreamer.

*And this final Dreamer must light the **Torch** and keep it burning with its violet flame, and break the giant's spell for good, so the Energy flows to both worlds, restoring memory to all and beginning a **New Magic Age**.*

'You're famous,' said Maybie shyly. 'The Ninth Dreamer.'

Jayben frowned, struggling to remember. 'When I first woke up, it was just after the Blue Moon, when the lights aligned, just as the Book said, and I had Rainbow

crystals in my hand. I remember Phee's dad – Tedrik – saying I must be the Ninth Dreamer, that I was the only one who could stop everyone's memories being wiped by Null, that evil adult Dreamer who always wears a mask. That nobody knows Null's real name, but he was able to harness the power of Free-Dreaming and somehow connect to his earthling, his Earth self. He's hungry for power and total control and—'

'And he believes that *he* is the Ninth Dreamer of the Book,' finished Peggro.

'Yes,' said Phee, 'and those idiots, his followers, still believe it. No one even knows who Null is. He just hides behind a mask, so he can pretend to be whoever he wants.'

'He has great powers,' Captain Winnibar said seriously. 'The first adult to ever become a Dreamer – that must have taken some serious northern sorcery! Until he came along, there had only been eight Dreamers, of course. And now it's all down to you, the Ninth. Null will stop at nothing to get the Golden Torch. He whispers a spell on the wind everywhere he goes and any adult who hears it becomes mindless and whispers the same spell too, spreading the curse to any adult listening – becoming nullheads. Only children are safe.'

'Yes, like our poor dads,' Peggro said. She smiled at Jayben. 'Any other questions?'

'Who are these Chordian Guards?' he asked. 'It's familiar, but . . .'

Phee explained. 'The Guard are the scholars sworn to protect the Dreamers of the Book. They'll be glad to hear you're awake, Jayben.'

Peggro nodded. 'Raynor has been keeping them updated. There's a whole network who will help us reach the tomb.'

'Do we all have earthlings?' asked Jayben. It was strange to think there was another version of himself, Ben, asleep somewhere right now.

'Yup,' said Maybie. 'Someone in the Earth World, who looks like you, born on the same day. The scholars said we all have an earthling self but our minds are never connected, unless our earthling sees a chord or something. And that's why every time you cross over, you've forgotten most of what happened. To get your memories, you need to see the full moon here.'

'Exactly,' said Phee, pointing to Jayben's head. 'But the Guard say it's all in there. Your memory and your earthling's, so don't worry. They're just locked up for now. But we know that you *can* remember a few things across worlds. That's how you Free-Dreamed the phone box. You told us you remembered being in a phone box with your mum in the Earth World.'

Jayben sighed. 'I don't understand why I can't control my powers, though. Didn't Raynor say that I'd basically gained them because I'd seen the almost-full moon here?'

'She said it unlocked your powers,' Peggro explained, 'but you still need to figure out how to control them. And to unlock all your memories, you need to see the full moon.'

'But when? How? The other Dreamers got all their memories back! They could remember their Dreams of Earth World – clear as day. That meant they only had to think of something from Earth World and they could bring it here.'

'So can you, Jay-Jay,' said Maybie. 'We've seen you.'

Jayben shook his head stubbornly. 'Not on purpose. Raynor is right – my powers are too wild and dangerous.'

'Well, you've unlocked the gateway,' said Phee soothingly. 'You just need to figure out how to open the door all the way. The more you can remember from Earth, the more control you'll have over your powers, I guess.'

Jayben nodded. 'Thanks. I guess I just need to practise.'

He ran his finger back over his chapter.

'If I'm the Ninth and Final Dreamer,' he continued, 'then it's all up to me. That's what the Book says. The world can't go on relying on Free-Dreamed objects for Energy. It's too fragile. I have to get the Torch back, light it – but this time *keep* it alight for ever, so that everyone has enough Energy to remember. So that the connection between the worlds is strong again and magic can return.'

'Easy peasy!' Maybie said with a giggle.

Then Russog let out another fart and said in a toddler's voice, 'Bum stink!'

Jayben couldn't help but laugh. 'Thanks for your help!' he said, wafting the air. 'But to keep the Torch burning, I need to break the spell the Book says a giant put on it. What sort of spell was it?'

Peggro shrugged, looking glum. 'Well, if we knew that . . .'

Jayben turned to the end of his chapter, the last page of the Book, and felt a familiar sting of frustration to see the blank page, one of the eighteen missing pages throughout. Every chapter had at least one blank page. He would have given anything to know what they said. He couldn't shake the feeling they were important somehow.

But there were one hundred and thirty-eight pages that *weren't* missing, he thought. They covered over five hundred years of Elf World history, the stories of his eight famous predecessors. Surely there must be some clues as to how he could fix the Torch.

He flipped back to Chapter One.

The First Dreamer

Sojan was the First Dreamer and her wise words had helped him a lot in the darkest of times.

If it's not impossible, then you can do it.

He read the famous quote again, words that had become his own mantra. He needed them now more than ever. Every one of these eight Dreamers had tried to break the giant's spell on the Torch, to light the Torch and keep it alight, burning continuously like it had done all those centuries ago. Perhaps one of them had come close?

He read page seven, the final page of Sojan's chapter.

Yes, the giants were powerful but often careless. The northern witches complained that giants were

*just as clumsy when attempting their spells, always forgetting to protect their curses from **the skeleton key words**. Skeleton key words are simple phrases that can undo the spell. For reference, these words are*

He turned over to a blank page and sighed heavily. He had forgotten that page eight was the first missing page.

'Yeah,' said Phee, 'you always found that first blank one annoying.'

Jayben gritted his teeth. 'They're *all* annoying. This page had the skeleton key words on it – a phrase that could have undone the giant's spell on the Torch! Look, Sojan says they never bothered to protect their spells against it.'

'I'd never heard about a skeleton key,' said Peggro, looking worried. Peggro didn't like not knowing things. 'I thought there were loads of different phrases that witches and wizards use to unlock their spells.'

Captain Winnibar leant in, scratching her eyepatch. 'There are, but there's also the skeleton key,' she said. 'That's the master key. It can pick any lock, undo any curse. The words are closely guarded, though. Many a witch I've tried to shake them out of, to no avail.

They all swear on their sorry lives that those words were forgotten generations ago.'

'But the Book was written six centuries ago,' said Jayben, 'at the end of the Magic Ages. The ancient scholars predicted every single Dreamer – including me. So if anyone discovered the skeleton key, and wrote those words down, it would be here.' He felt tingles in his gut, like he just knew it. 'If I can just find that first missing page, then—'

Phee laughed. 'Find it? Ben, the original Book was found in the ruins of Formadon, in the Livid Isles. Ya know – after a volcano erupted?'

'If the Book survived all that,' Jayben persisted, 'then it's possible the missing pages did too. And if they are somewhere then they can be found, right? Maybe the Chordian Guards will have some ideas. I'll ask Raynor.' He looked around at the doubtful faces. 'It's worth a try, isn't it? These words could break the curse and save the Torch.' He rested his fingers on the blue charm on his wrist. 'And with a bit of luck . . .'

Captain Winnibar shook her head. 'As the great Seventh Dreamer once said, Jayben: *You won't need luck if you refuse to lose.*'

He smiled at her. Then he was distracted by a particularly bright bookshelf behind a glass screen.

There were dozens of bookles clustered around it. 'What's special about that book?' he asked, pointing to it.

'Ah,' said the captain, leading Jayben and his friends to see. 'This, dear boy, is the precious Free-Dream we have aboard the *Beth Rose*. It gives off enough Energy to keep our minds sharp when we're far out to sea.' She unlocked the glass door and shooed away the bookles to reveal a tattered little book with a faded cover. 'It was gifted to this ship by Junas, the Seventh Dreamer, well over a century ago. It radiates enough Energy for my entire crew.'

Jayben was fascinated. 'If this is a Free-Dream, then it must be a book from Earth World?'

He looked more closely at it and saw the title.

The Little Mermaid

by

Hans Christian Andersen

Captain Winnibar nodded. 'Swapped for a measly book of spells. It's quite the fishy tale – pun intended.'

The Little Mermaid. Jayben didn't recognise the

book but as he read the title he felt strange, like he'd heard it before. Was it a memory? *A memory from Earth?* He felt hope balloon inside him. Something was stirring. If his memories returned, then maybe he'd control his power – the power to Free-Dream Earthly objects. He needed his powers if he was to face Null in just four days—

BANG!

The deck shook. The ship leant hard to one side, and the chairs slid across the room, crashing into the bookshelves.

'What's happening?' cried Jayben as the bookles hid away, dimming the library. The shells had stopped singing and the crew could be heard yelling from below.

Captain Winnibar rolled her eyes, anchoring herself to a shelf with her hook and putting the precious Free-Dreamed story back behind glass. 'For the love of old Moonie!' she said. 'I can't leave the helm for a moment!'

A man came bursting through the door. 'HESSEGROL!' he yelled, with a look of sheer terror.

The captain laughed, dragging herself to the door as the library tilted to the other side. 'Really, lieutenant? A hessegrol, in these waters? Have you been at the bad rum again?'

Then came an ear-splitting roar and an eerie hiss, and the whole ship was shaken back and forth, knocking the books from their shelves and throwing Jayben and his friends to the deck.

'Oinff! Oinff!' said Russog, burping nervously as the beams began drumming and the shells began singing again, faster and faster. Phee strapped him into her backpack.

Winnibar stopped laughing and looked at Jayben. 'Although, given our new passenger, a hessegrol might make sense. Stay here, kids,' she told them, taking her sword from its sheath.

Jayben felt his stomach drop and his heart quicken. 'It's happening,' he said to Phee, as they shielded themselves from the falling books. 'I'm causing the nightmares again!'

CHAPTER 7

The Grim Head of the Hessegrol

Jayben could hear the crew screaming above the deep roar and the loud hissing. 'What the heck is a hesse-hessegr–'

'Hessegrol,' said Maybie, crawling under one of the chairs. 'A big sea monster, from Nomolia.'

'But what's it doing this far south?' said Peggro. 'They only live in warm waters.'

'It's me,' said Jayben. 'Remember the darkning storms? They're a northern thing, you said. But they happened in Wenden, in the south, because of me.' He remembered the fierce beasts they had faced: the ferocious skallabore he had saved Tedrik from; the mighty grannix he had stopped, before it could get to Peggro and Maybie.

But I stopped them, he realised. They had been calmed by him, somehow. He had seen more behind their eyes than violence. Every animal, however fierce, was once a baby. And every animal must nurture their young. He had seen that side of them and he found their wildness a thing of wonder.

He could hear the screams of the crew's children – and he made up his mind.

'Whatever a hessegrol is, it's here because of me. Which means I have to stop it.' He grabbed the empty bookshelf and pulled his way along the sloping deck, to the door.

'But the captain said to stay here!' said Peggro. 'It's too risky!'

'We can't let him go alone,' said Phee. She tightened Russog's straps in her bag and hurried after Jayben, with Peggro and Maybie following reluctantly.

The ship was bending and the staircase was now blocked by twisted beams. Jayben gritted his teeth and noticed a hatch to one side with cold air whistling through a crack. He grabbed the icy handle, took a deep breath and flung it open, staggering on to the open top deck.

In the moonlight, he could see the crew slipping about at the foot of the central mast, waving their swords at something that stretched across the width of the deck. Jayben shuddered in the cold, blasted by a salty spray from the crashing waves.

Raynor came running towards him, but the motion of the ship sent her skidding on to the side. 'Get back inside!' she yelled.

Jayben kept staring ahead. As his eyes adjusted to the darkness, he saw black scales slithering like a gigantic snake – it was the width of a carriage. The creature was coiled around the ship, contracting and crushing the decks together. And then he saw it. The grim head of the hessegrol.

There was something canine about its head; it was like an enormous hyena – although he wasn't sure how he knew what a hyena was. Something tugged at his memories from the Earth World.

The hessegrol had a square jaw full of jagged teeth, each the length of Jayben's forearm. Its black nostrils dripped with mucus. Its ears pointed forward, and its red eyes stared straight at him, before it let out a deafening roar, showering him with globules of drool and fish bones.

'Over here, jelly brain!' Captain Winnibar yelled

from the rigging, shooting a spear at the creature's neck. It barely pierced the scales and the beast simply ignored her.

Jayben took a step back, but the creature swept towards him, as though seeking him out. He felt a surge of energy coursing through his veins, just like when he'd faced the grannix last year. *I can do this again*, he thought, slowing his breathing. He remembered his calm face reflected in the skallabore's eyes. *I just need to be brave again. To see more in their eyes than violence.*

'Come away!' shouted Raynor.

Ignore its eyes and teeth, thought Jayben, relaxing his shoulders and standing tall. *Look at its cool black scales and its red gills. I bet it can swim really deep. It's amazing!*

The hessegrol hissed, flicking its forked tongue only a few feet from his face. Jayben didn't blink. He held its gaze and held his breath.

One . . . two . . .

Jayben rubbed his eyes and stared up at a ceiling of crooked beams. A white shell was humming a mellow tune. It was glowing in golden sunlight from an open round window. He felt exhausted and his whole body was tingling. He couldn't remember falling asleep in this bed.

'What happened?' he whispered, slowly trying to sit up. As he moved, the bed swung to one side, tipping him on to a pile of pillows.

'*ARGH!*' he cried.

Phee's face appeared around a door. She was clutching a book. 'Thought that might happen.' She knelt down beside him. 'Sorry about the hammock. They're the only beds they have here. You okay, Ben?'

Jayben said nothing. His body felt heavy and he was utterly confused. He noticed that the ship wasn't drumming now. He looked to the open window and saw a clear blue sky. He couldn't hear the waves crashing, just a quiet *whooshing* as the room rocked gently. And the air from outside was warm.

Where were they? How long had he been asleep? He noticed that his shadow on the deck was long. Was it morning or evening?

'It's okay,' said Phee, putting her hand on his shoulder. 'How's your head now?'

Somehow he was now wearing shorts and sandals, and a thin white shirt. 'Where are we?' he said, fighting down panic.

'You don't remember today, do you?' Phee asked gently. He noticed that she too was wearing shorts and sandals, a lime-green summer shirt and her loaded toolbelt.

Jayben stared blankly, trying to recall, but there was nothing since the bitter evening when he'd faced the sea beast—

'The hessegrol!' he gasped. 'What happened? Is it gone?'

'Try to relax,' Phee said. 'I'll explain everything. You had a seizure this morning so I guess you've forgotten a lot of last night, plus anything from today as you've been sleeping it off. That's normally what happens when you have such a big seizure. Not surprising after everything you went through yesterday. And yes, thanks to you, that horrible thing swam off.'

Jayben sighed with relief.

'That was yesterday, Ben. It's early evening now and we're getting close to Fellooz. We need to make a short stop—'

'We're stopping?' he interrupted. 'But we don't have

time! The eclipse is in three days now and we need to get to that tomb before Null does!'

'We're stopping,' said Phee firmly. 'To get you some medicine.'

Jayben frowned. 'But I already have medicine, don't I? I remember drinking a tonic every day when we lived in the woods.'

'I know – we brought it with us, packed it in a trunk and put it in the carriage. But the carriage plunged into the ice before we got to the ship, remember? It was in there.'

Without his medicine, Jayben could have a seizure at any time. Shaking, he shoved his hand into his pocket, pulling out his precious black compass. That, at least, was safe. He read his parents' words engraved into the wood: *As long as you have a home to find you will never be lost*. His eyes filled with tears.

Phee gave him a hug. 'We're going to Maybie's home – it's nearby. She says her grandma might have something that can help you, until Raynor can get the same tonic you were taking before. We'll be back on track in no time. Okay?'

Okay? Jayben *wanted* to pretend that everything was okay, to force all the emotions back down. He checked his pocket again, feeling the hard edge of the yellow star glass gem. It was there, in one piece. That was something.

Phee was still looking at him with a worried expression.

'Yep.' He nodded. 'I'm okay.'

'Oinff!' Russog appeared, jumping on to Jayben's lap and licking his face. 'There there, little one,' he said in Larnie's soothing voice. Russog always knew what to say, even though he was using someone else's voice.

Jayben scratched his green fur and felt comforted by his cheeky wet snout.

A purple hat with turquoise feathers poked through the doorway.

'Is that a fierce young Dreamer I hear?' Captain Winnibar squawked, hobbling in and offering her hook to help him stand. 'I told 'em you'd bounce back, kid! I said, anyone who can stand up to a hideous giant mutt like that won't let some ailment keep 'em down. Not without a fight.'

Jayben grinned at her twinkling eye and stood up straight.

'Wasn't that a riot?' Winnibar cackled. 'I haven't had the thrill of fighting one of those in quite a few moons. Feared them since I was a girl, but you won't catch me surrendering!'

'Is the ship all right?' he asked.

'A little bent.' She shrugged. 'It'll take more than some overgrown sea-pooch to sink this old gal, I'll tell you that. And thanks to you, Jayben, not one of my crew got so lucky as to escape this mortal coil.'

Jayben couldn't help but laugh. He was relieved that the ship and the crew were unharmed. But without the crystal shilling, he knew that the hessegrol wouldn't be the last nightmare on their journey to the tomb. 'We might not be so lucky next time,' he said, clutching his Trollwood charm.

The captain shook her head. 'Like I told you, dear boy: *You won't need luck if you refuse to lose.*'

'Here,' said Phee, handing a book to the captain. 'I finished reading this.' Jayben realised it was the tattered old copy of *The Little Mermaid*.

'What d'ya make of it?' asked Winnibar.

'The mermaid turned to sea foam in the end,' said Phee. 'Hmm. I did not see that coming.'

The captain cackled again, playfully knocking Phee in the shoulder. 'Crazy old place, that Earth World must be! People with fishtails? No, thank you!'

Maybie came bounding through the door, wearing a canary-yellow summer dress. 'I think it sounds magical!' she said. 'I hope my earthling is a mermaid.'

Phee laughed. 'You can fly, Maybie. Pretty sure that beats living underwater.'

But Maybie had noticed Jayben was awake and she rushed over to him. 'At last!'

'Nice to see you better again,' said Peggro from behind her. He was wearing a sky-blue shirt, shorts and sandals. 'Are we there yet?' he asked, nervously buckling his satchel and fiddling with the burble worms on his wrists. 'I know your family don't quite live on dry land, Maybie, but *anything* would be better than *this*.'

They heard a whistle from outside and a chorus of bells ringing.

'We're here!' said Maybie, taking Jayben's hand and leading him through the door. 'I can't wait for you to meet everyone! My family had to build new homes after they fled Zamar and – well, you'll see. It's quite special!'

The others followed. Jayben stashed his compass and star glass back in his pockets, as Captain Winnibar threw open a door to hot sunshine.

They were back on the top deck of the *Beth Rose* but it couldn't have been more different – not a snowflake in sight. Jayben took a deep breath of the warm sea air, gazing at the sails in the blue sky, flapping about in the gentle evening breeze. It was hard to believe that only yesterday he had been shivering on the ice.

'Good to see the colour back in your cheeks,' said Raynor, patting Jayben on the shoulder. She was wearing shorts now too, with a red vest. 'You did a brave thing yesterday, Jayben.' She lowered her voice. 'I know you'll be worrying – I'll find you another shilling in Fellooz.'

Jayben swallowed and nodded. 'I just have to keep everyone safe till then.'

She squeezed his shoulder. 'Come on,' she said. 'Let's take this one step at a time. The first thing is to try and get you some medicine.'

Jayben nodded and as he turned to go, Maybie tugged at his shirt. 'I think you should hang on to this one,' she said, handing him her map, neatly folded. 'Just in case we get separated. I have a spare in my room.'

'Thanks,' he said, carefully stashing it in his pocket with his compass.

They looked down over the side of the ship. Jayben was surprised to see no land, but instead a cluster of enormous toadstools, dozens of them, bobbing gently on the calm water. Beneath each toadstool there was a floating living area on a platform, and they were all connected by narrow floating walkways. One toadstool sheltered a kitchen; there were a few armchairs beneath another. It was like a small village on the sea, anchored to these strange giant toadstools, gently swaying on the surface.

Jayben felt the deck of the ship beginning to vibrate his feet. It was softly drumming the alarm and the shells had started singing again.

Captain Winnibar tossed a stepladder down to the platform and her crew gathered on the deck. 'We'll wait here for you, Jayben,' she said, as the shells began to sing.

'Thank you,' said Jayben. He already felt attached to Winnibar, her crew and the ship, but he was glad that he would no longer be putting them in danger.

A call came from the platform below and Jayben looked down to see a short man wearing a white sunhat, vest and shorts. 'Welcome, Ninth Dreamer!' he said, cheerfully waving as others gathered around the ladder.

Jayben took a deep breath and waved back.

He tried to pretend that he wasn't about to make their worst fears come true.

CHAPTER 8

A Tiny Face in Every Teacup

Jayben stepped down from the ship's stepladder on to the floating wooden platform. Maybie quickly joined him, running ahead to one of the giant toadstools that was jingling with hundreds of windcharms. She ran into the arms of a short woman who wore a coral dress and a matching flower in her curly black hair. She had brown eyes and brown skin, and wore large pearl earrings and bracelets and a golden Fairywood charm around her neck. All around them, others were wearing those same charms.

'Mamma!' said Maybie gleefully. 'Meet my friends!'

The woman smiled warmly at them all. Jayben liked her already.

'Welcome home, baby,' she said, kissing Maybie on the cheek, 'And welcome, friends. We've heard so much about you.'

'Any of it good?' joked Phee, carefully crossing the swaying platform with Russog snorting on her back.

Peggro followed, looking anxiously at the sea lapping at the edges. 'Is this where your family moved to after Zamar came?' He hurried under the nearest toadstool to steady himself against its stem.

'Yes,' she said, her face clouding over. 'We'll stay here until it's safe again.' She pointed to some orange bumps on the horizon, the distant shore in the light of the setting sun. 'That's Fellooz. The whispers have spread everywhere.'

Raynor joined them. 'Not to mention the threat of Zamar and his men. Ever since Null sent him there to overthrow the local leaders, the people have lived in fear.'

Maybie's mother shook her head at the distant coast, then turned to Jayben with another smile. 'We're safe here. My name is Fancie. Now, first things first. I understand you're in need of a tonic? Right this way . . .'

Fancie led Jayben and the others through the cluster of toadstools and open-air living areas until they reached one with a large kitchen beneath it. There were mismatched wooden cupboards and counters in various bright colours, and a long kitchen table loaded with bowls of fruit.

Maybie pointed to a tiny old lady with pink hair, snoozing in a rocking chair. 'That's Gan-Gan,' she said.

Peggro hugged the toadstool stalk in the middle of the kitchen. He couldn't take his eyes off the water, which was sloshing about in the gap between the edge of the kitchen floor and the living room it was chained to. 'How are these huge stools floating?' he asked.

'Oh, they're not floating,' said Fancie. 'Their stalks go all the way down to the sea floor – they're pretty sturdy. They make a good anchor for our life here, for now, till we can go home.'

Suddenly something small fluttered into the kitchen and crashed into a hanging pan. It was a tiny boy, no more than four inches tall, with four silver wings on his back. It reminded Jayben of how small Maybie was when she shrank down to fly – something he knew that all Fairywood children could do.

'Poor bubba,' said Maybie with a chuckle, cupping her hands to catch the boy. 'I told you, aim for the sink until you can land properly.'

'Oinff! Oinff!' said Russog, wriggling about in Phee's bag, his green snout outstretched, clearly longing to chase the fairy. Then he said sternly, in Tedrik's voice, 'Leave them be, Stinkbomb!'

The boy giggled, then flew past Jayben and through a curtain.

'That's Dunno,' said Maybie, 'my baby brother. He's only five. His flying is coming along.' She grinned as three more miniature flying children swooped into the kitchen, dropping little sacks of nuts on the table, before whizzing behind the curtain. 'And those are my cousins.'

'Calm down, Russog!' said Phee, taking off her backpack and distracting him with a nomseed. His tongue was flapping as he panted in the heat.

Maybie filled a bowl for him from a bottle of fresh water.

Fancie took some glass jugs from a cupboard and rang a bell. 'Gan-Gan is still asleep,' she said, 'so Wilsie will come help you with the tonic.' She put a few berries into each jug. 'Let's fix you a nice cool tea first. Help yourself to the cups.' She pointed to the shelves of crockery.

Jayben went to take a blue teacup – when he saw something wriggle inside it. A tiny face of white fluff with pointy ears and big black eyes popped up, blinking up at him.

Maybie laughed. 'Not *those* cups, Jay-Jay. Unless you want mee-mow hair in your tea!'

He realised that there was a tiny face in every teacup.

'Miss me?' said Maybie, stroking each of them on the head in turn.

'Mee-mow!' they said in unison.

'They're too cute!' said Phee, struggling to contain Russog.

A slightly bigger mee-mow popped out of a spotty teapot with a yawn, licking its paws.

'Evening, Nanny Bean,' said Maybie. 'Nice nap? Jay-Jay, you can stroke them if you like.'

Jayben brushed his finger over Nanny Bean's ears.

'Mee-mow,' she said, rubbing her silky-soft head against his hand.

Peggro, however, seemed slightly apprehensive, pointing to the wings on their backs. 'I read that mee-mows are related to hemniks?'

Raynor snorted. 'About as much as you're related to Null.'

Jayben grinned. Mee-mows were nothing like the

aggressive hemniks he had encountered. They were pretty adorable, he thought. Then he noticed that one cup in the pastel-coloured tea set was empty. 'Was there one in there?' he asked.

'Never for very long,' said Fancie, unscrewing a jar of red sweets. 'You won't catch Lulie Bean napping. She's got to be everywhere. But she can't resist candy – she can smell it a mile away.'

As she removed the lid and rustled the sweet wrappers, a blur of white fluff came speeding through the air and crashed into the jar with a loud, high-pitched 'MEE-MOW!'

Maybie laughed, tugging the ball of fluff out of the jar, its paws gripping one of the sweets, its wings beating so fast they were almost invisible. 'She's my one,' said Maybie, gently smooshing her face against the furry creature. 'Lulie Bean, meet my friends.'

Lulie Bean pounced on to Jayben's shoulder and began licking his neck.

Fancie poured tea for everyone into some other cups and Jayben took a big gulp. It was refreshingly cold and sweet, like the juice at Phee's house. He looked up to see a teenage girl crossing the water from the living room, carrying books under her arms and a pencil tucked behind her ear. She was much taller than Maybie, with her mother's black curls, brown skin and brown eyes behind her glasses, and she wore a purple blouse and shorts.

'Here comes my big sis, Wilsie,' said Maybie, running to give her a hug.

Wilsie put her books on the table. 'Glad to see no frostbite on you from up south.'

'Nope,' said Maybie, 'but we did get chased on to some thin ice by some very angry Agents.'

Wilsie wrinkled her nose. 'For *real*?'

'Yup,' Maybie said, 'but then we escaped on to a big magical ship. Oh! And then we were attacked by a HUGE hessegrol.'

'A *hessegrol*?' asked her mother, dropping a bowl on the counter.

'Brave Jay-Jay made it go away. But then he got poorly again.'

Fancie squeezed her daughter in a tight hug. 'I'm so glad you're all here now. Wilsie, Jayben needs a tonic for his head.'

Jayben downed his tea and passed Lulie Bean back to Maybie. The mention of the hessegrol reminded him how much danger he was putting everyone in, simply by being here. He needed his medicine – then he'd have to go.

'This way,' said Wilsie, leading Jayben and his friends out of the kitchen and further through the maze of conjoined floating rooms. Peggro nervously followed, staying close to Phee and Raynor.

'Mind your step,' said Wilsie, as they crossed a weathered plank to the final platform. Beneath this last toadstool was a broad cabinet, filled with black bottles. Wilsie selected a few of them, then opened a box of what looked like dried leaves, emptying them on to some brass weighing scales.

Jayben was intrigued. 'You know how to make medicine?'

'Well, the basic elixirs. I was still in school when we left Fellooz, and Gan-Gan only has books on the old spells, from the Magic Ages. No good to us, unless Maybie gets her magic back again, from being close to you.'

'Oh, I hope so!' said Maybie, looking at Jayben. 'I was starting to learn tricks after you came into your powers, Jay-Jay. Then my charm stopped glowing and I couldn't do it any more. But maybe now that you're awake again . . .'

Jayben bit his lip. His powers were strong – but beyond his control. He gazed at the distant coast of Fellooz on the horizon, glowing red in the final rays of the sun. Could Raynor find another crystal shilling for him there?

He walked around the cabinet to see the calm water gently lapping at the edge of the platform where an old fishing rod rested. He could see a white sofa, with two people sitting on it. Then he froze.

'What the—' he cried.

The people were *tied* to the sofa, Jayben realised, with a prickle of horror. Their mouths were bound by white face masks and their eyes looked straight at him, staring blankly.

'Oh, I should have warned you,' said Maybie. She didn't look surprised, just sad. 'That's my poor pappa. And my Auntie Snazzie. They were nullheaded.'

The white face masks were moving ever so slightly, like the pair were mouthing something but Jayben couldn't hear or see what. The whispers. Null's terrible curse. Jayben had a sudden memory of Tedrik shuffling mindlessly into the night as Jayben screamed internally, *Tedrik! Come back! Please, Tedrik! Come back!*

Null's curse was the cruellest because it robbed people of everything they held dear. All those precious memories of home and family and love – gone. Jayben knew that pain, and he knew cruelty too, deep inside.

He had experienced it in the Earth World, he was sure of it.

It sent a flare of anger shooting to the surface.

'It's so unfair,' he said, taking Maybie's hand. 'It has to stop. *I* have to stop it.'

The anger was growing, he could feel it. His chest grew tight – and then in his mind he saw something black, and the old fishing rod in front of him started to shake and glow.

CHAPTER 9

Who is Low Battery?

CRACK!

In a bright flash of light, the fishing rod turned into a tablet.

I've seen that before, thought Jayben.

'WOW!' Maybie gasped, as the others came running round to see the tablet lying on the platform. 'You did one again, Jay-Jay! A Free-Dream! But . . . what *is* it?'

'Oinff! Oinff!' said Russog, managing to writhe halfway out of Phee's backpack.

Jayben's head was spinning, but he knew one thing – for the first time today he felt excited by his powers, not just afraid of them. He'd Free-Dreamed something from the Earth World!

'It's a tablet, I think,' he said, crouching down to see that its screen was lit up. The tablet had a half-removed sticker reading:

Property of Milgrove
Manor School

The words seemed familiar and so too did the world displayed on the screen, in which everything was made of little cubes.

Peggro and Wilsie were speechless, mouths gaping.

'Is that a picture of the Earth World?' said Phee, eyes wide.

Jayben shook his head, 'I think it's a – game?' he said, intrigued to see a character with a square face. He reached down but before he could pick the tablet up, it flew into his hand.

The blue square charm on his wrist was glowing. The Trollwood magic of his ancestors was back. Suddenly the strange cubic world was replaced by a red flashing screen and a warning:

LOW BATTERY!

And, just like that, the screen went black.

'Who is Low Battery?' asked Phee. 'I know a Low, back home, in our class. Is the machine trying to contact someone called Low?'

Jayben shook the device and tried pressing the tiny button on its side. Nothing happened. But that didn't matter – the tablet working wasn't important. What *was* important was that *he'd* brought an object from Earth World here, for the first time since his long sleep. It was proof of his Free-Dreaming power – he just needed to learn how to control it.

Now he felt a little less afraid of facing Null. 'I hope you didn't need that fishing rod,' he joked.

Maybie squealed. 'Magical! Do you think the mermaids in Earth World look like that too? All made of squares?'

Raynor chuckled, shaking her head. 'Earthlings are like our twins, aren't they? As far as we know, they look exactly like us.'

Peggro sniggered. 'Yes, and how many people have you met with fishtails, Maybie? Let alone square ones!'

'All right, you two,' said Phee. 'But this is awesome, Ben. You can do it! Just like before. You can face Null, and this time we can stop him for good.'

Raynor nodded, her expression becoming serious. 'Phee's right, Jayben. This is a good sign. Once you can control these powers you'll be more than able to stop Null—'

'Look!' interrupted Maybie, holding out her wrist. Her own charm was glowing. 'My old magic is back too! But how?'

'You were holding hands,' said Raynor. 'Just like before, Jayben's powers must have drawn the old magic from your blood.'

'My turn next, okay, Ben?' said Phee with a cheeky grin. 'I can't wait to be super strong again!'

'Well,' said Peggro with raised eyebrows. 'I *won't* be holding your hand, Jayben. To be honest, I'm not sure I liked it when I went invisible. It was weird.'

Jayben laughed, nudging his nervous little brother.

'But it was amazing, Peggro!' said Maybie. 'And just think what we can—' She stopped, distracted by a noise from the white sofa. She turned around and gasped. Her father's brown eyes were blinking at her, his bushy eyebrows raised. His mouth was moving behind the face mask, but now they could hear muffled words, not whispers.

'Pappa?' said Wilsie softly. She rushed to him, tugging his face mask away to see a broad smile.

'Wilsie?' he said, and a tear ran down his cheek. 'Maybie?' His eyes streamed. 'What happened?'

'PAPPA!' the sisters cried together, quickly untying him from the sofa. Then they noticed that their aunt was trying to speak too. 'Auntie Snazzie!'

'Girls?' the woman said with a gasp as they removed her mask.

Jayben felt dizzy with joy and relief. 'They're cured!' he said, turning to Phee, Peggro and Raynor, who were all beaming. 'Just like the nullheads at Last Rock, when I lit the Torch. But . . . I didn't use the Torch here.'

'You unleashed quite a burst of Energy when you did that Free-Dream,' said Raynor, putting her hand on his shoulder. 'Enough to break the spell for them, apparently. Well done!'

Maybie's dad shook Jayben's hand. 'Thank you!' he said. 'I can't believe it!'

Maybie's aunt gave him a big hug.

Jayben was thinking fast. 'If I could break the spell for them with a Free-Dream, maybe I could do it again. Tedrik, my dad . . . they might remember who they are too, inside. We just need to find them first. Their memories might still be there, just locked away – like mine.' He hesitated. 'Even though I don't exactly know how I managed to do it this time.'

'Your powers will come, Ben,' said Phee, 'and your

memories. Everything from your earthling's mind too. You'll be able to Free-Dream whatever you want, whenever you want. Once you've seen your chord again.'

Raynor raised a hand. 'Let's not get ahead of ourselves. The important thing is to get to the tomb in Fellooz before Null. To keep him away from the star glass gems, until after the eclipse. Even if Zamar gets the Torch to Null, his powers are too weak to control it. Getting to those gems under the light of the eclipse is Null's one chance to regain his power. We cannot let that happen.'

Jayben nodded, feeling emboldened. 'You're right. But if I can learn to control my powers, we can take the Torch back too. We know the curse on the Torch *can* be broken – we just need those skeleton key words. I'll break the curse, light the Torch for good this time *and* make sure that nobody forgets ever again.'

The others were silent. Phee looked excited, Peggro nervous, Maybie admiring. Raynor looked, as always, a bit worried.

Jayben took the large yellow gemstone from his pocket and glanced at the horizon, to the Felloozian coast, dimming in the twilight. It wasn't far. Three days would be enough, wouldn't it? *I can do it.*

As he looked into the distance, he spotted a few specks of light at sea, in the early dark. They seemed to be getting closer, and fast. He remembered the Agents who had chased them from Wenden and his stomach lurched.

'Who is that?' he said, stepping away from the side. 'What if someone's seen the chordian light that I'm giving off?'

Russog hastily dived back into Phee's bag.

Wilsie came closer and frowned at the approaching lights, then laughed. 'Don't worry. Those aren't Agents. It's just the others back from fishing. They're noisy, but harmless.'

Jayben sighed with relief to see that the lights were being held by a dozen teenagers, each one riding a kind of tub, pulled by a large fish. They all looked friendly and were holding long sticks with a large pea tied to the end, dangling in front of the fish.

'Pappa?' said the tallest boy, dropping his lantern and pulling his reins as he reached the platform. His eyes were wide with amazement. 'Are you . . .'

'Shrugg!' said Maybie's father, as the boy leapt from his tub and into his father's arms. 'Everything was blank and then suddenly I could remember!'

'Auntie!' said Shrugg, hugging them both. His aunt

still looked dazed. 'You're back! But how? After all this time?'

'I'll explain,' said Wilsie, taking her aunt's arm. 'Let's go and tell Mamma!'

'We need to celebrate!' said Maybie, following her sister on to the next platform, back the way they'd come.

Shrugg quickly retrieved his lantern from his tub and fed the dangling pea to his fish, before hurrying after his sisters, followed by their teenage cousins, barely noticing Jayben and the other visitors in all the excitement.

'Here,' said Raynor. She handed Jayben the small glass bottle of medicine that Wilsie had made for him. 'One spoonful, Wilsie said.'

He quickly poured the prescribed spoonful and popped it in his mouth. He gagged. It tasted vile, like bad black pepper mixed with the worst morning breath ever. But anything was better than the worry of having another seizure and he managed to swallow it.

'Listen, Jayben,' said Raynor gently. 'I know how exciting this must be for you – being able to Free-Dream, release people from Null's curse. But your powers are strong and you don't yet know how to use them. Null is a powerful enemy. Don't let this go to your head – and make sure you take this medicine.'

Jayben nodded seriously. He knew that Raynor was right. All the same, he couldn't forget that thrilling rush when the fishing rod had disappeared . . .

They walked back towards the family kitchen. One by the one, the giant toadstools started to glow as night fell, until the entire floating village was gleaming gold, bobbing gently in the warm evening breeze, beneath the deep-blue sky.

The party had already started. Some of Maybie's cousins were playing drums and woodwind instruments, and her father was dancing on the table with Fancie. Families were setting down dishes of food. As the evening wore on, Captain Winnibar's crew joined them with barrels of rum and cooled cropple cones for the kids.

'We heard the good news, Dreamer,' she said, ruffling Jayben's hair. 'Freeing Null's prisoners already!'

Maybie's father raised his cup for a toast. 'To the Ninth Dreamer!' he said, patting Jayben on the back. 'That dark menace stands no chance against you!'

Jayben grinned. He needed this tiny moment of joy, knowing that it couldn't last. For Raynor's words echoed in his ears. And beneath the singing and the cheering he could hear the tapping from the furniture and the low drumming from the beams of the anchored ship. He recalled Tedrik's words. *That's no music, lad . . . The trees are warning us.*

They were sounding the alarm about *Jayben*.

He pushed the thought away. Tonight he needed a break, and he tried his best to only hear the music.

CHAPTER 10

The Sinking Village

Jayben dreams a new dream.

He stands in a desert of golden sand, reflecting the blinding sunlight. He's in the shade of a tree, by a pool of water. In front of him there is a brown suitcase, open, and inside it are a few pieces of paper, gently flapping in the breeze. He bends down for a closer look . . .

Suddenly he's in a dark cave of shadows and screams. There are heavy footsteps behind him. Somehow he knows it's a monster and it's hunting him. He runs. His heart's pounding. He smells smoke and feels heat, and a flame flashes from behind. He can see a faint light ahead. The monster is getting closer. He can hear screaming—

'*HELP!*'

Jayben woke in a cold sweat, breathing fast. He bolted up in darkness, seeing only a dim beam of moonlight between two curtains. The glow of the toadstools was gone and the air was cooler now.

He'd definitely heard a scream.

'HELP US!' somebody shouted.

Jayben leapt from the quilted floor where he'd been sleeping and threw open the curtains to see the platform opposite sinking below the water. Some of Maybie's cousins were jumping from their half-submerged beds on to his platform. The giant toadstool above them had turned grey and was shrivelling down into the sea, taking part of their home with it.

Jayben reached out his arm to help one of the girls to safety, only to feel water sloshing around his toes. He turned around with a start and saw his toadstool was now grey too, its cap crumbling. It smelled like it was rotting.

He grabbed the girl's hand and they jumped to the next platform, a sitting room. The table and cabinets were beating the alarm. The chairs in the next room were drumming too, faster and louder, and the kitchen counters were frantic.

In the dim light, he saw Peggro emerge from another

curtain, looking scared. Phee appeared, cradling Russog, who was shaking.

Maybie ran towards them crying, 'This can't be real! It's a nightmare!'

Jayben's heart raced. This was a nightmare – the nightmare of all the Fairywood folk, to lose their homes a second time. He knew it was happening because of him.

There wasn't time to think. All he knew was that he couldn't put his friends and family in danger any more.

'I have to go!' he said. He squinted into the darkness to the end of the village. The tubs that had carried the teenagers were still there. He checked his pockets, relieved to feel the bottle of tonic, his compass and Maybie's folded map. But where was the star glass gem? He looked back through the curtains and let out a sigh of relief. It was there, next to his pillow. As if responding to an unspoken call, the gem flew through the air, into his hand. Jayben's square blue charm was glowing on his wrist.

'Incredible!' said Peggro, impressed in spite of the danger they were in. Then he blinked. 'Jayben, what are you doing?'

But Jayben had taken off, running and jumping

from platform to platform, between the shrivelling toadstools and panicked villagers, who were clinging to their drumming furniture.

'Go to the ship!' Jayben yelled to the villagers, rushing past Raynor, who was helping people to safety. 'Raynor, get everyone aboard the *Beth Rose*!'

'But what about you?' she asked, but Jayben didn't look back, sprinting to where Maybie's brother's tub was moored, still attached to the large fish. In the tub there was a bucket of peas. Jayben quickly grabbed one, attached it to the end of the rod and held it out. The fish immediately started sploshing about, trying to reach the pea, and Jayben jumped into the tub.

'Wait for us!' shouted Phee, hurrying after him with Peggro and Russog, who was back in Phee's backpack.

Jayben hesitated. He wanted their help, but not as much as he wanted them to be safe. Going to an unknown realm by himself to face Null was terrifying. But he had no choice. He had to be brave. He had to be the boy who looked into the eyes of fierce beasts and saw goodness in them.

'I'll be okay!' he shouted back, then clenched his teeth, grabbing the reins. 'You'll be safer here without me. Get to the ship!' He untied the tub from the platform and aimed the rod to the right. The fish jerked right and swam forward.

This is it, he thought grimly. He was on his own.

As he sped away from the sinking village, though, he felt the tub dip. He spun round to see that Phee and Peggro had scrambled in behind him.

'I thought I said—'

'You need to listen more!' Phee snapped, struggling to sit upright as they rocketed through the water. 'You don't remember everything from last time. We learnt an important lesson: we're stronger together. We're not leaving you.'

'No way,' Peggro whimpered, clinging to the sides of the tub as it was struck by the waves.

Jayben took a deep breath. 'You know what this means?' he said. 'It'll be like last time. All your worst fears could appear – your nightmares – and we might not be able to escape them.'

Phee lifted her chin and nodded. After a moment, so did Peggro.

Jayben smiled. 'Okay, then. Thanks.'

He couldn't pretend he wasn't glad to have their support – and besides, there was no time to turn back. He could see the distant shore on the horizon, glowing pink now as dawn broke, and they could already feel the air heating with the first rays of sunlight.

The tub tipped side to side as the fish swam faster, and Peggro gagged. 'I forgot the burble worms!' His face turned green, then he retched over the side.

Phee rubbed his back. 'It's not far, Peggro,' she said, 'not at this speed!'

'Which way is the city of Zamar?' asked Jayben, delving into his pocket for the map, leaving one hand firmly on the reins. 'The tomb is just outside the city, right?'

He heard a little voice from behind: 'Straight across the desert!'

He looked around to see a miniature Maybie, flying on four silver wings, no more than seven inches tall, wearing an identical yet tiny version of her canary-yellow dress and carrying a matching yellow sack full of her regular-sized things. 'Go, Jay-Jay!' she said cheerfully, tightening her charm necklace.

'Maybie!' cried Jayben. 'You came too! And you're flying again!'

'You didn't think I'd let you go without me, did you?' she said in her small voice. 'Don't be silly, Jay-Jay! My family will be fine – they've escaped worse than a few sinking mushrooms.'

Jayben couldn't help but grin, glad to have his funny, optimistic friend along too.

Then there was another noise to his right: 'Mee-mow!'

He turned to see a tiny, white fluffy face with big black eyes and pointy ears, flying alongside.

'Lulie Bean!' said Maybie, buzzing over to her pet. 'Why do we even have a teacup for you when you never stop flying?'

'Mee-mow!' she said, licking Maybie's face and buzzing ahead.

'Well, now that we're all here—' Jayben broke off as he felt a sudden chill in the air.

THUD!

A wave beside them turned to ice. The big fish swerved out of its way.

Everything went black for a moment, like a flash of darkness.

THUD!

Another patch of water froze solid, shattering against the tub like glass.

The fish panicked, sploshing uncertainly between blades of ice.

'Darkning!' Jayben cried, seeing his breath in the air and remembering the awful storms, brought on

by his powers. They snatched all Energy, wherever they struck.

Maybie and Lulie Bean swooped to Jayben's shoulder and Russog hid on Phee's back.

'There's no escape!' cried Peggro, before heaving again.

Another flash of black.

THUD!

'It's okay,' said Jayben, pulling back the reins, now covered in frost. He forced himself to stay calm and think. 'Darkning never stays in the same place twice, remember? You told me that, Peggro. So we need to stay where it just struck.'

But the fish wouldn't stop and the wind was picking up, building angry waves around the floating shards of ice.

Jayben tried to stay focused, looking forward at the approaching coast. 'We're almost there!' he cried. 'We just need to—'

His words were drowned out as a powerful wave rose up from behind, tipping the tub and plunging them all into the sea.

Jayben held his breath, desperately trying to see the others through the haze of bubbles as he furiously kicked to get back to the surface. The needles of ice melted in the warm, crystal-clear water. As the bubbles scattered, he could see a colourful seabed below, only a couple of yards down.

But where were his friends? His head resurfaced and he gasped for air, looking left and right for any sign of them. Then another wave hit and he was forced under once more.

CHAPTER 11

The Forest of Giant Cacti

Suddenly Jayben wasn't swimming. He was lying on a bed of sand and he could breathe again. He opened his eyes to a clear blue sky and sat up, his heart racing. The foam from a wave delicately lapped at his sandals. Somehow the sea was calm again, no sign of any darkning, and he was safely on the beach, soaking wet but warm in the hot sun.

Over the swooshing waves, he heard Phee.

'Ben? You all right?'

'I think so,' Jayben said, not quite ready to move. 'How are the others?'

A reassuring 'Oinff!' came from Russog and a groan from Peggro.

133

'We made it!' Maybie cheered, still in her miniature form.

Jayben sat up to see her standing on a pebble, trying to restyle her wet hair, while comforting her soggy pet mee-mow.

'We'll soon dry off, Lulie Bean,' said Maybie, straightening her dripping-wet wings.

Jayben laughed, giddy to see them unharmed, waggling his finger in his ear to get the last drops of water out. He could still taste the salt from the sea. Then he noticed the big fish stranded in the sand, still attached to the upturned tub, and still trying to reach the pea on the rod.

'Hang on!' he said, rushing to free it. The others came to help detach the reins from its head. Jayben and Phee carefully lifted it, carrying it back to the sea.

'Thanks for your help,' said Jayben, as it slid into the water. He fetched the bucket of peas and flung them all in. The fish happily gobbled them up and swam away.

Jayben checked his pockets. The gem, map and compass were still there. He took the soggy map out and unfolded it on the warm sand.

'So whereabouts are we?' he asked Maybie.

'Well, that's the Fairywood,' Maybie explained,

pointing inland to some tall cacti growing along the coast in both directions, as far as the eye could see, 'so we must be a little further west now.'

Peggro pointed to the Fairywood on the map and frowned. 'A *little*? If we're at the Fairywood then we're a hundred miles off course!'

'Hmm,' said Maybie, vibrating her wings as they dried in the rising sun. 'I suppose so.'

Phee let Russog down. 'I guess if you can fly, then that's not that far.' She gazed at the Fairywood with a grin. 'I've always wanted to see this place. I've never seen a forest without actual trees before.'

'So to get to the tomb,' said Jayben, holding out his compass, 'we need to head north-east, right? Through the woods?' He was intrigued by the strange plants of the Fairywood. 'Is this forest where your ancestors lived, in the Magic Ages?'

Maybie nodded with a smile. 'Our family has always been here. They lived in Karassan – the city in the woods. Before Zamar came along. I'm glad you're here in winter. The flowers are so beautiful. In the summer it's too hot to go outside.'

'It gets hotter than *this*?' said Peggro, wiping the sweat from his brow. The air was getting warmer as the morning wore on.

Phee laughed nervously. 'We'll manage. I came prepared for this.' She took a bottle from her bag, removed the cork and dabbed some white cream from it on to her hand, rubbing it into her face, arms and legs. 'Summer gel, Ben,' she said, handing the bottle to him. 'Remember?'

The sweet, nutty smell of it seemed familiar, and he was happy enough to copy her and slapped a generous amount of the oily lotion on himself.

'What if Zamar's men see you, Maybie?' he asked.

She shook her head. 'Us kids come back here all the time, to get food. Unlike grown-ups, we can shrink and fly. And we're immune to the whispers.'

Jayben sighed, remembering the floating village shrivelling and sinking. 'Now it's not safe for them at sea either. All because of me.'

Phee shook her head, crossing her arms. 'All because of *Null*, you mean. They wouldn't be out there at all if it wasn't for his curse. None of this is your fault, Ben. You're the one who can help.'

Maybie agreed. 'That's why we've come with you. Now, let's get into the woods.' She took flight, with Lulie Bean at her side. 'There'll be some shade there and it'll hide your light a bit.'

Jayben, who was all too aware that his chordian

light was a beacon to any Agents with chordical lenses, couldn't wait to get into the cover of the forest. He offered to carry Maybie's yellow sack of things for her, and they hurried up the beach.

Then Peggro stopped suddenly, checking his pockets. 'My moondial!' he gasped. 'It's not here! How will we know the date?' He turned to look back at the waves, his expression worried.

Jayben glanced back and saw a glimmer of silver on the wet sand. *The moondial!* As the thought entered his mind, Peggro's moondial came flying through the air and into Jayben's hand. 'So cool!' Jayben grinned, handing it to his little brother. 'That's my Trollwood power, right? Summoning things?'

'Anything made of metal or rock,' said Peggro, stashing it back in his pocket. 'Like the old trolls, remember? From Mum's side of the family.' He tapped the blue glowing Trollwood charm on Jayben's wrist and smiled shyly. 'And thanks, big bro.'

Jayben smiled back. He felt sad that he couldn't remember their mum or dad – but at least he had found his funny, clever, permanently worried brother.

'Magical!' said Maybie, leading them into the forest of giant cacti.

The straight green plants towered over them, dotted

with brightly coloured flowers and covered in long, sharp spikes.

'Careful, Stinkbomb!' said Phee, grabbing Russog by the collar to stop him bounding into the needles. The whooshing of the sea was replaced by a gentle hissing sound that seemed to be coming from the plants, joined by cheerful chirps from something up high.

They walked quietly for a while, Maybie flying alongside them, deeper into the forest. Jayben was looking at his compass to check that they were heading north-east when he tripped on a root and looked up to see an actual tree. Like the cacti, its trunk was green and straight but it had helical branches twirling in all directions, laden with golden nuts, just like the one Maybie wore on her neck. There were also dozens of jars hanging from the branches, in all different colours, filled with little keepsakes.

'A helicorn tree!' said Jayben, spotting some fallen gold nutshells by the roots. 'Like the helicorn trees in the Giantwood; the trees we keep memory jars on. But this looks a bit different. Is this the Fairywood kind?'

'Yup,' said Maybie, handing him one of the nuts. 'Full of the spirits and memories of fairies from the old, old days. But the poor Jarmaster of this tree had to flee Zamar's men, like us. Come on, Jay-Jay, it's this way.'

They walked on, further into the woods, and then—

Jayben looked down to see he was sitting on the hot ground. His shirt was soaked with sweat but the air felt cooler and the hissing had stopped. His head swam. *What just happened? Was it another seizure? Where were the others?*

CHAPTER 12

That's Not a Plant!

Jayben heard a buzzing to his left – the sound of Maybie's wings.

'Jay-Jay?' she asked, sounding concerned. 'You okay? You were walking and then you just . . .'

Jayben tried to answer, but he couldn't. *It was happening again.* Another seizure. He couldn't move. He just kept staring down at his knees.

It was a horribly familiar feeling – heavy and fuzzy and like he was somehow outside of himself. Trapped.

Phee's sandals appeared and she knelt down beside him. 'It's all right, Ben,' she said softly, and he felt her hand on his shoulder. 'It'll be over soon.'

And then, just like that, Jayben was free.

He could move again. He looked up and saw Lulie Bean hovering by Phee's silhouette in the low sunshine. Phee smiled, which helped a little.

'I think it was an absence seizure,' she said. 'What's the last thing you can remember?'

Jayben fought down panic. 'Where's my brother?' he blurted, hoping the sight of Peggro would help.

'I'm here,' said Peggro, appearing to his right. Jayben felt his breathing slow. It *did* help. Seeing his brother and his best friends by his side was enough to steady him.

He trusted them. He knew that if they were there, he could cope with just about anything.

It didn't make the seizures any less scary. It didn't seem to matter how many he had, they were still terrifying. He didn't know when the next one would come, just that it would, and that he was completely powerless to stop it.

'Why didn't the tonic work?' he asked through gritted teeth. Hot tears spilled down his cheeks and he wiped them away.

'Maybe it's not the right medicine for you,' offered Peggro.

'Or perhaps it just takes a while to work,' suggested Phee. 'Maybe you need a few doses.'

Maybie fluttered in front of Jayben's face, licked her tiny hands and held them over his forehead.

'What are you doing?' he asked.

She smiled. 'Hopefully this time I can make your head better, now that I've got my magic again.'

Glowing specks appeared in her palms then passed into his head.

Jayben didn't feel any different, but he smiled anyway. 'Thanks, Maybie,' he said as she removed her hands.

Peggro rolled his eyes. 'You tried that before, remember? Why would it work this time, when it didn't before?'

'All right, Peggro,' said Phee, crossing her arms. 'She's only trying to help.'

Maybie shrugged. 'It can't do any harm.'

'You don't know that,' Peggro muttered, protective of his big brother. 'Nobody knows enough about old magic. It could be dangerous.'

Phee gave Peggro a sharp look. 'Honestly, worry, worry, worry. Can we not do this *now*?'

Suddenly there was a disgusting eggy smell and Russog appeared. 'Who farted?' he said in Tedrik's voice. He jumped on to Jayben's lap and began licking his chin with his green snout. Then in Larnie's gentle, lilting voice he said, 'There there, little one.'

Jayben couldn't help but laugh and he gave Russog a big hug.

Phee looked around at the tall green cacti. 'It's going to be dark soon and Ben needs a rest. We're gonna have to camp here, guys. Though I don't know how. We've got no tent.'

Maybie flew up high. 'I think I saw a bell-bush ahead. That'll make a good shelter for a little rest.'

Jayben gazed up at the deep-blue sky and sighed. The one solitary wisp of cloud was turning orange as the sun was winding down. Then he had a nasty feeling. 'How long did I miss?' he asked.

Phee helped him up. 'It's evening. You've forgotten one day. Still two sleeps before the eclipse. Try and relax.'

'*Relax?*' said Peggro, fanning his sweaty face with the folded map. 'How can we *relax*? We've been walking in the sun all day and haven't even reached the desert yet. Without Raynor, we have no help from the Chordian Guard and there's only two days left to the eclipse!'

Phee scowled at him, but Maybie giggled. 'Silly Peggro. We're gonna be fine. We'll have a quick rest, Jay-Jay, then when the moon's up we can keep going, when it's nice and cool.'

Jayben stood carefully. His muscles felt weak. 'Just a quick rest. Yes.' He checked his compass, staggering forward. His legs were like jelly and his mouth was bone dry. 'Anyone got some water?'

'Yup,' said Phee, passing the tin bottle from her toolbelt.

Peggro quietly sniggered, 'You're lucky we stopped Phee from draining a cactus earlier for water. They're deadly poisonous.'

Phee rolled her eyes. 'Okay, thanks, Professor Know-It-All. At least I had the tools for draining it, once Maybie had found us the right kind of plant.'

Jayben hesitated, bottle at his lips.

Maybie giggled. 'It's safe, Jayben. You drank some earlier, remember?'

He didn't remember but he trusted them and he was parched. He took a big gulp from the bottle. There was a bitter, grassy aftertaste, but it was water, and his whole body felt cooler from one mouthful.

He followed the others onwards, gawping up at the cacti around them, stretching into the sky.

'Mind the needles!' said Phee, as Jayben narrowly missed getting spiked in the leg.

He watched the brightly coloured flowers, which seemed to be getting more fluorescent as the sun was

setting. Then he stopped, intrigued. One of the cacti had no flowers.

'Interesting,' he said, reaching between two of its spikes to put his hand on its waxy green surface. It was gently throbbing. In the dimming light, he noticed some other flowerless cacti, making eight in total.

'What a weird plant,' he murmured.

Maybie frowned, hovering – and suddenly shouted, *'That's not a plant!'*

The cactus jolted, knocking Jayben on to his back. Stunned, Jayben looked up to see that the columns were *moving*. They spread out, revealing a body and head, with eight big black eyes and two extremely long fangs.

It was like a giant green spider, camouflaged in the cacti.

'KRIZZARD!' Maybie screamed. 'RUN!'

Jayben jumped to his feet and fled with the others through the dense forest. He could hear the cacti being ripped apart behind him as the immense krizzard chased after them, tearing through the plants and sending needles flying. His body buzzed with adrenalin. He heard a high-pitched squeal and looked back with horror to see Russog writhing on the ground with a long spike through his front paw.

'RUSSOG!' he cried. Everyone stopped. The krizzard

was gaining fast, only yards away, but there was no way Jayben could abandon Russog. Without hesitation he hurried back and scooped the injured skoggle into his arms.

The others waited behind him, trembling.

'I've read about these,' gasped Peggro. 'I always thought they sounded like a complete—'

'Nightmare,' finished Jayben grimly.

The krizzard was gaining on them. Jayben realised they could never outrun it, not through such a tight maze of deadly needles. He'd never even heard of a krizzard, but he knew it was an animal, and the only option left was for him to face it, just like he'd faced so many fierce beasts before.

He turned to face it. Confused, the creature paused too. Then it continued its approach, but slowly, warily. As though it was stalking him.

There was something about the way its legs moved that gave Jayben the creeps. It really was like a colossal spider, covered in thousands of lethal needles. Behind its serrated fangs, its mouth was foaming, and from its belly came a deep groan.

'Jayben!' cried Phee, running back to grab his arm. Peggro followed, eyes on the creature. 'What are you doing?'

He glanced around frantically. To his right there were some fallen spiky branches. Could he use his power to throw them at the beast with his mind? He imagined them soaring through the air to the target. But nothing happened. *Only works on rocks and metal*, he remembered.

His only hope was to tame the creature as he had others before. The problem was, he was terrified.

The creature edged closer, crushing the spikes underfoot.

'Here.' He passed Russog back to Phee, breathing in and out as slowly as possible to steady his nerves, as the creature neared, shaking the ground. There was nothing left to do but try and be that brave boy again. 'I have an idea.'

Peggro was clinging to his big brother's shirt. 'I think any idea that isn't running is a very bad idea.'

Jayben could hear Maybie's wings buzzing close by, and Lulie Bean too.

'I could shoot it, Ben,' said Phee, loading her fishdart.

'No,' he said. If they were to stand any chance, he needed to appear calm. 'Its skin is tough and it's huge! You'll only make it angrier. Stay here, guys. It'll be okay.' He unpeeled Peggro's hand from his shirt and slowly took a step forward, relaxing his shoulders.

'Ben, are you sure?' said Phee, trying to calm Russog, who was still whimpering.

Jayben took another step.

The krizzard stopped, clearly puzzled, cacti falling all around it. Then, as though making up its mind, it lurched forward. It was only feet away now and in the twilight Jayben could see himself in the two larger eyes on the beast's hairy face.

He held his nerve as the creature loped towards him. *I can do it again*, he thought, remembering the moment when he'd faced the hessegrol. *I can be brave. Just . . . ignore its legs and its fangs. Look at its two biggest eyes. Look at its furry face. It's almost . . . cute?*

The krizzard raised its fangs.

Jayben held his breath, staring into the two biggest black eyes without blinking.

One . . . two . . . three . . .

The krizzard paused. Then it blinked, dropping its fangs and closing its mouth.

Jayben didn't dare breathe yet.

The groan from the krizzard's belly became a soft purr and its two larger eyes seemed to widen, as if looking at a friend.

Jayben exhaled with relief. He felt the urge to stroke

it. He smiled and slowly raised his arm, and the krizzard didn't flinch.

'Hi,' said Jayben, gingerly stroking the hair between its eyes.

The krizzard's purr became rhythmic and it rubbed its head against his hand. It smelled faintly like leather, which reminded Jayben of the stable at Phee's house, back in the Giantwood.

Maybie whispered, 'Jay-Jay, you did it again!'

Lulie Bean boldly buzzed forward and fluttered around the krizzard's face.

The krizzard suddenly jerked its head back, twitching from side to side. Peggro yelped and jumped back.

'It's okay!' Jayben said. 'These are my friends.'

The krizzard gave another jerk and then—

SPLAT!

It sneezed all over them.

CHAPTER 13

The Dome of Web

Jayben laughed with relief. 'Bless you!' he said, wiping the krizzard's mucus off his arm.

'What the dimmits!' said Peggro, cleaning his glasses.

Phee laughed. 'I guess it's allergic to mee-mows.'

'Oh dear,' said Maybie. 'Come here, Lulie Bean.'

Then the krizzard tilted its rear end upwards. In the fading light, Jayben saw a thick line of web shooting from the krizzard's backside on to the nearest cacti.

'What's it doing?' asked Jayben.

Before anyone could answer, the krizzard turned slightly and shot another line. Then another turn, and another strand of silk flew through the air.

'It's making a nest,' said Peggro. 'I've read about this.'

'Of course you have,' said Phee, nudging him.

'Oh!' said Maybie with an awkward grin. 'It thinks we're its babies!'

Phee burst out laughing. 'Are you actually kidding me?'

'Adorable!' said Maybie, hugging Lulie Bean. 'Sort of. If it wasn't a krizzard.'

The krizzard then raised its whole body about ten feet off the ground and walked forward a few steps, suspending itself over their heads, continuing to build the nest. Turning and spinning, turning and spinning, until they were encircled by an enormous, perfect dome of criss-crossed web.

Jayben was fascinated. A memory came to him then – of a drawing he'd made at Phee's family home, the Fellers' house, a year ago – a roof with almost the exact same lattice pattern. Somehow, somewhere, he must have seen this before.

He looked up at the krizzard's dark-green underbelly. It was still now, having finished the dome of web. He couldn't see any movement, but the rhythm of its purring had slowed. It sounded more like . . . *snoring*.

'I think it's gone to sleep,' he said with a big yawn.

The adrenalin was wearing off, leaving him even more exhausted and heavy than before.

'Well, I guess we did want a shelter,' said Phee, still cradling Russog. Jayben realised the little skoggle was hurt from where the needle had pierced his fur.

'I'm so sorry, Stinkbomb,' he said, stroking Russog. Then he turned to Maybie. 'Can you fix him up?'

She nodded cheerfully. 'Sure, but just let me de-shrink first. Nobody look!' She untied her yellow sack of regular-sized belongings and grabbed Phee's bottle of water. Everyone turned away.

POOF!

There was a bright flash of white light and Russog jumped. There was Maybie, full size again. Jayben was still amazed at how Fairywoods could shrink and de-shrink. The yellow sack was in fact her larger dress. She walked to Russog, stashing her miniature dress into her pocket and knelt down.

'Poor bubba,' she said, licking her hands and waving them over his wounded paw. Tiny, glowing specks appeared from Maybie's palms and, just like that, the skoggle's leg was as good as new.

'Oinff!' said Russog, leaping up to lick Maybie's cheek, before singing in Larnie's voice, '*Breakfaaast!*'

Jayben laughed, then gave another yawn. 'Good to

know that food words are still your happy sounds, Russog.' He felt even heavier now and had to sit down. The ground was surprisingly comfortable. In all the drama, he hadn't noticed that the floor was now carpeted in thick, soft petals from the cacti flowers that the krizzard had torn down. The sand below it was still warm and he lay down. 'Sorry, guys,' he mumbled. 'Just a short rest and then I'll be okay to keep moving.'

'You need a proper sleep,' said Peggro, looking worried. 'You always need a long sleep after a seizure. The eclipse is at noon, the day after tomorrow. How are we supposed to get there in less than two days, and without the Guard's help? And we're still in the woods! It's even more ridiculous than last time.'

'Ridiculous?' said Phee, eyebrows raised. 'I'll tell you what's *ridiculous*. It's you moaning every—'

'Guys!' snapped Jayben. The last thing they needed was a quarrel. They both stopped and looked at him. 'You're both right, okay? The whole thing *is* ridiculous. Two days *isn't* enough time, but what choice do we have? It's going to take everything we've got, so we can't waste our energy arguing.'

Phee sighed and sat down next to him, scooping up Russog for a hug. 'Sorry, Ben,' she said. 'We're just fed up – of Null, of his curse, of everything. The last year's been really tough. I know it's been hard for you too. You're right. We have to focus on getting it done, as impossible as it seems right now.'

Peggro sat down on the other side and muttered, 'Erm. Yes. Sorry.'

Maybie settled next to Jayben, looking nervously left and right at the krizzard's giant legs. 'If it's not impossible, then you can do it,' she chirped.

They smiled at each other.

'So, how unusual is it for a krizzard to be so tame with people?' Jayben asked.

They all laughed.

'About as unusual as a hessegrol letting a ship go,' Phee joked. 'It's you again, Ben. You have some weird gift with animals. Like the skallabore you saved my dad from, and the grannix that was going to eat Peggro.'

'I've only seen a krizzard once before,' said Maybie, as Lulie Bean snuggled into her pocket, 'when I was little. It destroyed my uncle's house!'

Peggro nodded. 'They're infamous in these parts. There's more about them in here.'

He opened a small book from his bag:

THE WORST
MONSTERS
IN THE WORLD

He turned to the chapter titled 'Fierce Beasts of Fellooz'. Jayben realised that, as scary as it was that his powers had drawn the beast to them, it was also pretty cool that his powers had disarmed it and turned it into the most unlikely of allies.

Peggro flipped through the book. 'Now, where are the pages on krizzards . . .'

Pages. Jayben suddenly remembered something.

'My dream, last night!' he said with great excitement. Suddenly he felt less sleepy. 'I think I remember—'

Everyone leant in.

'A new dream?' asked Maybie, wide-eyed. 'What did you see?'

Jayben pressed his fingers to his forehead. The image wasn't clear. 'Pieces of paper? In an open suitcase, I think.' He paused and then there was more. 'In a desert. Yes. It was definitely in a sunny desert.'

'A desert in the Earth World?' said Phee. 'Or in this world?'

'I don't know,' Jayben said. 'But I have a feeling it

was a special dream. You know, like when I used to see the arch in my dreams last year.'

'Something the Moonmother wants you to see, perhaps?' said Phee. 'That's what Raynor said the arch dream was.'

Jayben recalled people talking about the Moonmother before, the old woman who the elves believe lives in the moon, writing the stories of every world.

Phee frowned. 'But why would the Moonmother want you to see pages . . .'

Jayben felt a rush of excitement. 'Of course!' He gasped. 'The *missing pages* from *The Book of Dreamers*! We thought that first missing page might have the skeleton key words on it – the words that could break the giant's spell on the Torch. What if they're *here*, in the desert? That's what the Moonmother is trying to show me!'

'In Fellooz?' asked Phee, taking some large brown nuts from her bag, each one the size of her fist.

Jayben shrugged. 'Why not? We just need to find them!'

Peggro snorted, unfolding the map. 'You do realise how massive Fellooz is, right?'

'Well, if it's somewhere,' said Jayben, inspecting

the enchanted map of moving images, 'then it can be found.'

'True,' said Phee, 'but remember what Raynor said. The important thing is stopping Null from getting to the tomb. Finding the pages will have to wait until after the eclipse.'

'You're right,' said Jayben with a sigh, lying down again. 'We need to get to the tomb before Null and Zamar. Need to stop him and get the Torch back if we can.' He glanced at Maybie. 'What's Zamar like? Apart from being a nasty piece of work.'

'He's a horrible man. We're lucky we escaped,' said Maybie, her face clouding. 'When he and his thugs came to Karassan and captured so many of us Fairywood kids, they didn't only take their wings. They melted their charms to make more gold jewellery for Zamar!'

Jayben was appalled. 'I can't believe anyone could do that. Where are those poor kids now?'

She looked down. 'No one knows. The rumour is some went to Zamar's city, but that was a long time ago.'

'Why the dimmits did they take them?' asked Peggro.

'Null told Zamar to take control of the Fairywoods. But because we can fly, and kids can't be nullheaded,

Null's Agents couldn't control us. So they captured us instead. All my friends.'

They all fell silent.

'Here,' said Phee at last, passing Maybie one of the large nuts. 'Your favourite.'

Maybie beamed, then shook the nut and gave it a good hard whack on the ground, cracking it in two.

The familiar sweet, buttery smell hit Jayben's nose and evoked a warm feeling, and happy memories of home in the village of Ampelwed, back in the Giantwood.

'Gribblenuts!' he cheered, cracking his open to see the soft filling fizzing and foaming into a steaming, nutty hot chocolate. He took a sip and noticed a cool white light from the woods. The moon was rising, and the vast dome of silk shimmered in its glow. The moon was so nearly full and Jayben felt a rush of goosebumps. A full moon was his chord – it had given him his powers. *Was he drawing some more power from it now?*

He hoped so. He needed all the help he could get. Then he wondered about the star glass in his pocket. He took it out and the yellow gem sparkled in the moonlight.

'Did this really appear magically?' he asked Maybie.

She shrugged. 'Maybe the Moonmother sent it to you.'

'Or maybe one of the Guards,' Phee suggested, 'knowing it could boost your power in the light of the eclipse.'

He wasn't sure but whatever the reason, the gem could bring him strength when he needed it most. He stuffed it safely back in his pocket.

'I bet you'll get your memories back soon,' said Peggro, his glasses steaming up as he sipped. 'When you see the full moon.'

'Mee-mow!' said Lulie-Bean, enjoying the pieces of buttery shell dropped by Russog as he demolished his own gribblenut.

'Oinff!' said the skoggle, licking hot chocolate off his green snout, then eyeing up Phee's shells.

Jayben grinned and raised his edible cup in the moonlight to make a toast. 'To the full moon!' he said. 'To doing impossible things.'

Phee, Peggro and Maybie tapped their gribblenuts with his, and Russog jumped and said in Larnie's voice, 'Charming!' – before letting off the most horrendous fart.

CHAPTER 14

The Beetle's Voice

Jayben laughed, wafting the air to disperse Russog's stink. 'I've missed your grossness,' he said, as Russog jumped into his lap for a belly rub.

There was silence for a moment as they sipped their gribblenuts in the cooling moonlit air. Despite all his worry, Jayben felt a swell of warmth. He was here, with his friends – and his family. For all his fears around what lay ahead, in this moment he felt safe.

'I still can't believe we're brothers, Peggro,' said Jayben, nudging his arm, 'and that we didn't know until that Miraclest Eve, when we met our grandma!'

'We've got a grandpa too, remember?' said Peggro. 'Grandpa Mandon, Mum's dad. Grandma Fay said that he showed up at her house after you went missing from your bedroom last year – not knowing you'd wandered into the woods, to be taken in by Phee's family – and he went off to look for you. And he hasn't come back. That was well over a year ago.'

Jayben felt guilty. He had woken up, confused, with only his parents' compass. He had run into the woods and found Tedrik. If he had just stayed where he was, then his grandpa wouldn't be lost. But there was no point dwelling on the past – he needed to focus on finding his family. 'Someone must have seen something,' he said.

Phee sighed, clenching her jaw. 'I'm sorry, Ben. We've searched as best we can and no one has seen him anywhere. Maybe the whispers got your grandad the same as they did your dad and mine. It's been a tough year, okay?'

'I'm really sorry,' he said, putting his arm on her shoulder. 'If only I could have woken up sooner.'

'It's fine.' She forced a smile. 'I'm sorry too. It must be so confusing for you, knowing you've lost another year, and then facing all this when you finally wake up.'

'But there's always hope,' Maybie chirped with a grin. 'I mean, just look at my dad! Until yesterday we never knew if he was coming back. We thought we'd lost him for ever.'

Peggro crossed his arms. 'Except that he wasn't lost, was he? He was at home the whole time. Unlike Phee's dad and my dad. And Grandpa. Totally different.'

'Well,' Maybie said, faltering, 'I only meant that—'

'Who knows where our dads might be!'

'I'm just saying,' Maybie continued, blushing, 'that you never know—'

'I understand,' said Phee, butting in. 'We *do* want to think positive, Maybie, but it's not easy. I'm glad about your dad – it's amazing! But we have to be realistic.' Her voice cracked. 'It's been a whole year. They could be anywhere.'

'That's if they're even alive,' muttered Peggro.

Jayben's stomach dropped. The thought of them never coming back was too much. Having only just learnt of his mum's death, he couldn't bear the thought of losing his dad as well – and Tedrik too, Phee's kind and loving father who had taken him in.

He remembered the red phone box by the frozen lake in the Giantwood, after he Free-Dreamed it from Earth, a year ago. And the memory of his Earth mum with him, inside it, when he was little – both of them giggling. He wondered whether it was possible his mum could be alive in the Earth World while gone here.

He remembered that at the end of every century – six years from now – those in the Elf World believed a miracle would be granted by the Moonmother. A miracle that would bend the rules of both worlds. Jayben had wished to her to grant him the next Big Miracle – to help him find his mother.

Perhaps there was an upside to being asleep for an entire year – he was a year closer to the Miracle.

He noticed then that Peggro's pocket was glowing white. 'Can I see the moondial?' Jayben asked.

Peggro took out the silver gadget. It was like a pocket calendar, the size of Jayben's compass. Its gleaming moonstone was encircled by silver dials, engraved with the numbers needed to tell the date, according to the Miracular Calendar.

Jayben rubbed his thumb across its glass face and read the three numbers that were glowing: 6 – 6 : 362

'So, now the Sixth Miracle in history will happen just six years, three hundred and sixty-two days from now?'

'Yup,' said Phee, finishing off the sweet sticky shells. 'A wish will come true for someone, if they're super lucky.'

Maybie gazed at the moon. 'Yeah. Who knows what magical, rule-bending event the Moonmother will choose to write into the big story – the story of the worlds.'

Jayben yawned and handed the moondial back. There was so much to think about – but he was too tired. He rubbed his bleary eyes and pulled one of the giant petals to his chin.

Phee nudged. 'Not until you've had your tonic,' she said, in an almost parental tone.

'Oh, all right!' he said, finding the energy to pull himself up again, and taking the bottle of medicine from his pocket. There was no spoon to measure it so he poured a generous dose into the remaining half of his gribblenut, hoping that a few extra drops might be enough to stop his seizures. *Maybe the hot chocolate will help it taste better*, he thought, optimistically swigging it. Nope! Same awful peppery bad-breath taste. He gagged but he knew he had to swallow it if he was to stand any chance of being well. *Not that it's worked so far*, he thought.

'Here,' said Phee, passing him her water bottle.

He gulped down the cactus water. After the tonic, the grassy plant-water tasted almost sweet.

At last he could sink down against the soft petals on the warm sand.

Phee did the same, with Russog wedging himself under her arm, and Peggro shifted his satchel under his head for a pillow. But Maybie stayed sitting up, stroking Lulie Bean, who was snoozing in her hand.

'I think I'll stay up a while,' said Maybie, looking uneasily at the giant krizzard suspended above them.

'Fair enough,' said Phee. 'We can take turns.'

Peggro fidgeted, unable to get comfortable. 'What's that light in my bag?' he said, sitting up to investigate.

There *was* a white glow from inside, a warmer white than the moondial. He rummaged around, then pulled out one of his books to find a bookle clinging to the spine.

'A stowaway!' he said, holding it at arm's length.

Jayben and the girls chuckled. Russog raised his snout and said in Captain Winnibar's voice, 'Little nippers can't resist a new book.'

Maybie crawled over to see. 'It won't bite, Peggro,' she said. 'They're only interested in words. And sometimes they can even . . .'

She delicately stroked the creature's oval shell and it glowed brighter. Its shell opened slightly and, to Jayben's surprise, he heard Winnibar's voice again – but this time not from Russog:

'*The Orange Ghost of Orbago*,' Winnibar said softly. '*Chapter One . . .*'

Phee looked astonished. 'It must be a book from the captain's library. I didn't know bookles could mimic people like skoggles!'

Peggro looked just as surprised but then quickly straightened his face, nodding, as if he'd always known. 'Of course they can, Phee! I knew *that*. I – I've just never heard this story before.'

Jayben found his eyes closing, letting the beetle's voice – or Winnibar's voice – wash over him.

'*What do you see when you think of a ghost? Whatever it is, that will change once you've heard this story.*

A story that begins long before you were born, way back in the mystical Magic Ages . . .'

Jayben was intrigued, but he was too tired to stay awake to listen. He drifted in and out of sleep, catching snippets of the story.

'*. . . she said, and not for the first time . . . who lived at the top of a snoozing volcano . . .*'

Someone lives at the top of a snoozing volcano? thought Jayben. *I wonder how . . .*

But, try as he might, there was no fighting it, and he fell into a deep sleep and another dream.

CHAPTER 15

Zamar

Jayben is stumbling through a blistering-hot desert. He sees an oasis, a circle of trees around a pool of water. He hurries into the shade, where he finds an open suitcase filled with papers. He feels the urge to read them and bends down for a look—

And, just like that, he's back in that cave of screams and shadows.

The same heavy footsteps behind him. Jayben knows it's a monster. He knows it's hunting him. He runs, breathing fast, chokes on hot smoke as a flame licks his foot. He can see a way out ahead – a narrow chink of light. The monster is almost there. There's a bone-chilling roar—

Jayben woke with a start and scrambled to his feet. He looked up to see the krizzard's giant underbelly swinging back and forth. It jolted and gave another deafening roar.

'Ben!' cried Phee. 'What's going on?'

Jayben turned to see her standing and arming her fishdart.

Maybie, Russog, Lulie Bean and Peggro cowered behind her.

Jayben squinted in the early dawn to see that one side of the web was moving, like something was trying to break through. The krizzard became more agitated, stomping its huge spiny legs and turning to face the disturbance.

'Look out!' cried Jayben, as one of the legs thumped down beside Peggro, shaking the sand at their feet.

Phee grabbed Russog, Lulie Bean hid in Maybie's pocket and they all huddled together.

The krizzard gave another roar, and suddenly the web was torn open and a strange creature leapt through.

A crocodile? thought Jayben, seeing a long scaly head full of razor-sharp teeth. *Or a dog?* He wasn't sure if he was remembering such animals from the Earth World, but this was a mix of the two. It skidded on four grey muscular legs, before leaping towards the krizzard's face, barking and aggressively snapping its jaws. The creature sank its teeth into the krizzard, which howled in pain.

'A rawk!' shouted Maybie, diving behind Jayben as three more of the creatures bounded through the opening. '*Run!*'

Phee froze for a moment, trembling at the sight of these animals. 'I thought rawks were just made up in stories! I hate them!'

Jayben grabbed her, turning to flee, then stopped to see yet another kind of creature bursting through the opposite side of the web. Something black and much larger. Two immense, scorpion-like claws, four-hoofed legs, shiny black skin and four yellow eyes.

He knew this one. He and Tedrik had faced it together.

'Skallabore!' he shouted. But this one was different. It was covered in long scars, foaming at the mouth and wearing a bridle with chains from its back, rattling over a stub where it would have had a tail, linked to a two-wheeled golden carriage – no, realised Jayben, remembering the word: a *chariot*.

There was a man standing in the chariot, gripping the reins and a long whip. He was tall, muscular and bare-chested, with an orange tan and bright-blond hair. He wore black shorts and a chunky gold chain around his neck – as well as a purple monocle. Jayben recognised the monocle as the lens through which Agents could spy his chordian light. It had drawn their enemies, just as he had feared it would.

'Agent!' Phee shouted, her fishdart shaking in her hand.

'Worse!' cried Maybie. 'One of Zamar's men!'

The ground shook at his feet as the giant krizzard spun to face the skallabore, shaking the rawks from its face. As the silk web collapsed, Jayben looked with horror to see another black skallabore emerging from the cactus forest. Then another, and another . . . A total of six, each one pulling a golden chariot with a rider, and joined by a dozen more rawks, snarling and hissing.

As they backed away in fear, the krizzard leapt into action, lunging forward. The attackers skidded in the sand to avoid being impaled by its long needles.

'Hurry! The krizzard is going to buy us some time!' Jayben said. They turned and ran, fleeing through the krizzard's back legs, and into the cover of the cactus forest. 'What if it gets hurt?' he gasped as they ran.

'A krizzard?' said Maybie. 'Nothing hurts them!'

'We can't escape them,' cried Peggro. 'Not when they can follow your light.'

Peggro was right. 'We should split up,' Jayben said, pausing to catch his breath. 'My light is putting us all at risk—'

Phee groaned. 'This again, really?' she snapped, grabbing him by the arm. 'If you die, then *nobody* is safe. No one else can defeat Null – only the Ninth Dreamer. The Book said so. For the last time, Ben, we survived before because we stuck together. So come on.' She tugged him forward.

Jayben couldn't argue. As much as he wanted his friends to be safe, Phee was right.

They hurried on, further into the dense forest of thorns and flowers, radiant in the rising sun. To Jayben's relief, the barking of the rawks grew quieter.

Everyone stopped to catch their breath, dripping with sweat in the desert air. Jayben looked around for somewhere to hide but there was almost no vegetation between the straight, green column-like cacti, and their needles made them impossible to hide behind without getting hurt.

Phee passed around her water bottle. 'We'll have to keep going,' she said, fastening Russog into her backpack to get his paws off the heating ground.

'I never thought I'd be grateful for a krizzard!' said Maybie, giving Lulie Bean a few drops from the bottle. In the distance they heard the deep roar from the giant creature, and then—

BANG!

Everyone jumped at the unmistakable sound of a flashpin being fired.

BANG! BANG!

'No!' said Jayben, filled with dread as they heard the krizzard's roar shifting to a higher pitch. It sounded like it was in pain. He couldn't see anything for the woods. Then they heard the heavy stomps of the krizzard's legs. They grew fainter, like it was running away.

And then the sound of barking rawks again, and the rattling of chains.

Jayben hissed, '*Go!*'

They ran for their lives, the barking growing ever louder behind them.

'Oinff! Oinff!' Russog squirmed on Phee's back.

'Shush, Russog!' she said, and he stopped.

They could hear cacti snapping behind them, then the squeaking wheels of the chariots.

Peggro and Maybie were struggling to keep up. Jayben and Phee gripped their hands and dragged them along.

Jayben could see the fear in their eyes. They could

all hear the grunts of the skallabores and their pounding hooves.

They ran round an enormous cactus – and then, suddenly, there was only sky.

Jayben was at the edge of a cliff. 'STOP!' he yelled, and they skidded in the sand, halting right on the verge. His heart thudded as he watched Phee's fishdart tumbling from the ledge, down into a vast dry canyon, at least a thousand feet deep.

They backed away from the ledge, trembling. Then they froze. The sound of hooves, coming to a stop by the enormous cactus.

They turned. Their pursuers were only yards away. Jayben felt cold and hot all at once. Sweat ran down his dusty face.

Peggro was starting to hyperventilate, shivering next to him.

Jayben gave his little brother's hand a squeeze for comfort. He looked left to see two more of the skallabores emerging from the woods, drawing chariots. Then to the right. The other three were there too, aggressively snapping their giant claws. The pack of rawks appeared at their hooves, stopping before the cliff edge, snarling and opening their long mouths to show their jagged teeth.

Maybie started to cry. Phee whispered to Jayben. 'Now what?'

He couldn't answer. They were trapped. Could he tame these animals and somehow get them to help? He looked at the first skallabore, but it didn't look back. Its four yellow eyes were twitching left and right, up and down. He looked to the other skallabores and they were all in a similar restless state, foam dribbling from their panting mouths, their legs swaying under the heavy metal chains. The rawks weren't looking at him either, too busy snapping at each other. How could he connect with any of these creatures if they wouldn't look him in the eye?

He heard laughter from the men in the gold chariots. He saw one of them stepping down. Like the others, the man was tall, muscular and bare-chested, with the same orange tan and black shorts. But his short hair was jet black, and the gold chain around his shoulders was much thicker than the others'. As he stepped out of the cactus's shadow, Jayben saw a pendant around the man's neck, a gold letter: Z

Zamar.

Null's ally, the man who had kidnapped Maybie's people. He roared with laughter, looking down at them. 'Well, well. The Imposter Dreamer. I didn't think it would be this easy,' he said, taking a hand-held weapon from a holster. It had a wooden handle, a metal barrel and a trigger. *A flashpin!*

Phee shielded Maybie. 'What do we do, Ben?' she whispered. 'I dropped my fishdart . . .'

Peggro shut his eyes and squeezed his brother's hand tighter.

The flashpin's shiny barrel gleamed in the sun as Zamar slowly walked closer, light glinting off the metal.

Metal.

Jayben remembered what Peggro had told him about his Trollwood summoning magic. He had the power to summon *anything made of metal or rock*. But Jayben had never summoned anything except by accident before. Could he?

He focused on the flashpin and thought hard about wanting it in his hand, like he'd done with Peggro's moondial on the beach. It jolted, but it didn't leave Zamar's hand.

'Nice try,' Zamar smirked, tightening his grip and holding up his other arm to show the clanband on his wrist: a red pine-cone charm, glowing. Zamar had the super strength of the old Giantwoods. 'That weak

Trollwood magic won't work on me. Just come quietly.'

Zamar took a step towards them. Jayben swallowed and focused on the barrel, willing it to come to him. The weapon lurched in Zamar's hand. He held it with both hands and the weapon stayed. The veins on his arms tightened. His biceps were freakishly big, like he'd been weightlifting tree trunks.

One of the skallabores moaned and Jayben looked over to see it kneeling down, exhausted by its heavy chains. There was the loud crack of a whip, and the weary animal squealed, struggling to its feet again. For a moment it looked at Jayben and their eyes met. It was shaking, sweat streaming from its scarred face, against the chains of its bridle in the hot sun. The men laughed.

Jayben felt a rush of anger. To see a magnificent beast so mistreated and mocked, trapped as he had often been trapped . . . it struck a powerful chord inside.

He looked back at Zamar. The chunky gold chain on his chest shimmered in the sun and he noticed something familiar in one of its links, the exact shape of the nutshell around Maybie's neck. *The charms of the missing children.* He felt sick.

Again the crack of the whip, and again the skallabore whimpered. Zamar sniggered. 'Time we put that one down.'

Jayben's fury boiled over. He looked at the flashpin and it began to glow, violently shaking.

CHAPTER 16

The Chariots

CRACK!

In a bright flash of light the flashpin turned into a washing machine, knocking Zamar to the ground.

Jayben's eyes darted around, frantically searching for an escape. But there was none. Behind them was the cliff – and ahead, Zamar's men were advancing, wielding their flashpins. Zamar himself was howling with laughter. He stood up, uninjured, and gave Jayben a menacing grin.

'Well, that was unexpected, Imposter. But, as you can see, useless.'

What now?

As Jayben watched, Zamar grabbed the sides of

the washing machine and lifted it as though it was made of paper. His red Giantwood charm was glowing brightly. He began to squeeze the sides of the machine and it crumpled like a tin can, pinging shards of plastic, metal and glass everywhere.

Jayben should have been frightened by such a show of strength – but oddly enough, it gave him courage. There was nothing impressive about Zamar's cruelty. It was pathetic. Jayben clenched his jaw, thinking of those kidnapped children again, their wings removed, and looked at the crushed machine.

WHAM!

He sent the machine and Zamar flying back to the hooves of one of the skallabores.

Zamar sat up, looking less confident now. He looked almost scared.

Jayben stood up straight and boldly walked forward. Something had fallen out of Zamar's pocket. Something long and shiny and gold.

The Golden Torch!

Before Jayben could lunge for it, Zamar grabbed the Torch and held it tight.

Jayben stared, willing the Torch to come to him. He had to get it back. Then he heard Maybie scream from behind.

'Jay-Jay!' she cried.

He turned to see one of Zamar's men wrestling with her, trying to force handcuffs around her wrists.

'NO!' Jayben shouted. He looked back at the Golden Torch, opened his palm and, with a groan of fury, Jayben ripped it from Zamar's grip, into the air and into his hand.

'GET THEM!' Zamar yelled, but as his men raised their weapons Jayben said the words which came to him in a sudden rush of remembrance: '*Wish this.*'

BOOOOOM!

Flames erupted from the Torch, throwing the men to the ground and panicking the animals. In the blinding violet light, Jayben could see the skallabores turning to flee, taking the empty golden chariots with them.

'Come on!' he called back to his friends, and they ran as fast as they could, past Zamar, who was staggering, dazed, to his feet.

'Here!' cried Phee, jumping on to the back of one of the chariots, helping them all on, before the skallabore pulled it forward, back into the forest, reins flapping wildly.

'Aaah!' Peggro yelled, struggling to cling to the shaking carriage.

The skallabore galloped down a steep slope.

Jayben struggled to hang on with one hand, his other holding the blazing Torch. He caught a glimpse of two of the other skallabores, running away with empty chariots. He saw Phee and Maybie grinning in the brilliant light of the Torch and his hopes ballooned, feeling the golden spout in his hand once again, releasing wild bursts of Energy from the Earth World. *I can keep it burning*, he thought. *I just need those missing pages—*

BANG!

Everything sped up again. He looked back over his shoulder to see one of the men had made it on to a chariot and was catching up fast, firing his flashpin and whipping his skallabore.

Russog screamed in Maybie's voice, 'I wanna fly home!'

BANG! BANG!

Everyone ducked as pellets pinged off the rattling chains.

As the man reloaded his flashpin, Jayben stood up and pointed the Torch in the man's direction. Energy and light streamed from it. The man's skallabore panicked and took a sharp left, throwing him screaming into a cactus.

'Nice!' Phee cheered, as they raced on through the wood. 'Take that, you— Oh no, Jayben – look!'

One of the rawks was on their tail, barking and snapping its jaws. And there was another chariot through the trees to their right, driven by another of the men, aiming his flashpin.

BANG!

'For moon's sake!' cried Peggro, clinging on for dear life while keeping as low as possible.

The pellet hit one of the chains attached to the skallabore. It snapped, leaving just one chain attaching the chariot to the beast.

'Hang on tight!' Jayben shouted, as the chariot began swaying from side to side.

BANG!

Jayben felt a pellet fly past his cheek. *Too close!* He ducked lower. He was afraid to raise the Torch – there were so many cacti whizzing between them, the flames would catch the plants, and he couldn't risk starting a fire. *Then what?*

He looked around the inside of the chariot and spotted a pair of handcuffs on a hook. Holding the Torch up high, he grabbed them with his other hand. They were heavy and metal. *Metal or rock.* He turned back to the man, who was reloading his weapon as the skallabores galloped faster.

Could Jayben use his Trollwood power to *throw*

something with his mind? He'd seen Null do it. The man was ready to fire again. No time to think. Jayben raised the heavy cuffs, lining them up with the man. He thought of all those lost children again and—

WHAP!

The cuffs shot through the air, between two passing cacti, striking the man hard across the chest.

'AAAH!' the man yelled, losing his grip and falling into the sand.

Jayben exhaled with relief, amazed by his old Trollwood magic.

'The reins are breaking,' cried Phee as they swung to the right, the gold carriage scraping the side of a cactus. Jayben felt a sharp prod in his arm and looked down to see it impaled by a long needle, but he felt no pain.

'What the dimmits?' cried Peggro, turning pale. 'Jayben, are you all right?'

The Torch suddenly went out with a puff of white smoke.

Jayben saw his face reflected in the gleaming gold and brushed his finger over the indentations. It was back. *He* was back. Now he just needed those magic words, the skeleton key words. He was sure – well, almost sure – they were written on one of the missing

pages, and he could finally break the spell and light this Torch for good.

As he was lost in thought, a snarling rawk caught up, leaping to clamp its jaws around Phee's leg, its back legs dangling behind.

Phee screamed in pain.

'Get off her!' said Jayben, swiping it with the end of the Torch. It squealed, letting go and falling back into the dirt, disappearing behind them.

Maybie held Phee's arm. 'You poor thing!'

'I'm all right,' said Phee through gritted teeth. She raised a shaking finger. 'Ben, look!'

Jayben whipped round. They were hurtling towards a footbridge, crossing the canyon. It was nothing more than ropes and wooden slats, and barely wide enough for the chariot.

Jayben yanked the reins as hard as he could but the skallabore wouldn't turn. It raced on to the bridge.

'AAAH!' everyone yelled, feeling the bridge buckling beneath them and hearing lengths of rope snapping as the skallabore dragged them across, swaying perilously above the sheer drop.

'We're gonna die!' cried Peggro, shutting his eyes. 'This is it, this is it, this is—'

THUMP!

The skallabore's hooves crashed down on the other side, pulling them to safety, just as the ropes gave way and the bridge dropped into the chasm below.

Everyone stared at each other in disbelief. Against all the odds, they'd made it.

Gazing ahead of the skallabore's horns, Jayben saw the end of the woods, and beyond it nothing but sand to the horizon.

They thundered out of the cactus forest, galloping across the dust, until suddenly the chains broke, freeing the skallabore and flipping up the chariot, tipping everyone into the hot sand.

The creature stopped, breathing hard, sweat running down its flanks. It looked at them and raised its claws.

'No!' said Peggro, shuffling backwards.

Jayben looked the beast in the eye. It looked furious. Who wouldn't, after so much cruelty? The heavy chains, the lash of the whip, the cruel masters. It had been trapped. Jayben knew that feeling only too well, and how much the beast needed some kindness. It was panting in the blistering heat, the sun beating down on its weary armoured body.

'Hand me the water, Phee,' he said.

She quickly took it from her bag and passed it over,

never taking her eyes off the skallabore. Jayben could see that her leg was bleeding from the rawk's bite.

He slowly climbed to his feet, trying not to make any sudden movements.

The skallabore growled and stomped its hooves.

Jayben bent down and poured a few drops of water on to the ground. 'Here,' he said, standing back.

The skallabore stepped forward and lowered its head to sniff at the dampened sand. Then it looked up at Jayben.

'For you,' he said, holding out the bottle.

The skallabore opened its big, foaming mouth and Jayben reached out and emptied the water on to its tongue.

'Thanks for your help,' he said with a friendly smile. Tentatively, he reached out and gently stroked the horn of its nose.

The creature's breathing slowed. A moment of calm passed between them, reminding Jayben of the skallabore he had met in the Giantwood. Then the creature stepped back, retracted its claws and turned, before galloping away back into the woods.

Jayben laughed, giddy with relief. Exhaustion was also returning as the adrenalin wore off. 'Peggro, did you see— Wait. Peggro?'

To Jayben's astonishment, Peggro's head and hands were *invisible*.

'What?' cried Peggro, his voice coming from thin air, his glasses hovering. 'What's happening?'

'Your old magic!' Jayben cried.

'Seriously?' said Peggro, reappearing and checking his hands. His green Dragonwood charm was glowing. 'How come?'

'You were holding on to Ben,' said Phee, holding her wounded leg, 'when he Free-Dreamed that thing by the cliff.'

'Magical!' Maybie cheered, licking her hands and holding them over Phee's leg. 'Now for another kind of magic . . .'

The glowing specks appeared again, and in moments Phee's skin was fully healed. Maybie repeated the trick on Jayben's arm. Peggro turned green to see the long needle popping out of Jayben's closing wound.

'We made it,' breathed Jayben. 'And look what I've got!' He held the Golden Torch out to his friends and everyone smiled, allowing themselves this moment.

'We mustn't forget about the tomb,' Phee reminded Jayben. 'The Torch will make you powerful – but nothing can stop Null if he gets his powers back.'

Jayben nodded. He needed to remember that. But the powers the Torch gave him were intoxicating.

'Those guys were horrible,' he said.

Maybie shuddered. 'I thought they were going to catch me and put me with all the other kids,' she admitted. 'They're monsters!'

'And super gross,' said Phee, pretending to gag. 'All those veins. Listen, I think we need to keep moving. Zamar is still out there and he knows we're here.'

'But the bridge is gone,' said Maybie.

'There must be other ways to cross,' said Jayben, 'and we can't ever let him have the Torch again.' He put it back in his pocket, feeling its reassuring weight. Then he took out his compass. 'The eclipse is at noon tomorrow – it's still early morning. We can do this.'

He said the words firmly, hoping that it might make their impossible task somehow possible. But, squinting at the broken chariot in the dazzling sun, sweat dripping from the end of his nose, there was no escaping the harsh ordeal they were about to face. Trekking on foot across the vast desert was the only way to get to the tomb of star glass gems, and they had no water, no shade and precious little time.

CHAPTER 17

Candy in the Desert

Jayben stopped looking at the busted chariot and took out the map. He needed to focus on the plan if he was to stay positive.

'Okay,' he said. 'So we're at the eastern end of the Fairywood.' He ran his finger across the desert, past a moving image of a krizzard, to the east coast and the city of Zamar. 'If the star glass tomb is just outside Zamar, then we need to keep heading east, right?'

'But it's nearly two hundred miles away!' said Peggro, wearily wiping the sweat from his glasses. 'Across the desert!'

Phee was rubbing generous blobs of summer gel

into her legs. 'It's the only way, Peggro,' she said, handing the bottle around. 'We can make it.'

'But we gave the skallabore the last of the water!' Peggro continued, using a book to fan himself, with the bookle still attached.

'There's a traveller's shelter not too far from here,' Maybie said reassuringly. 'It'll have shade, and condensation cans full of water. We can rest there soon. I'll make sure we don't miss it.' She wandered behind the chariot and started her fairy sneezes.

If it's not impossible, then you can do it, Jayben thought, composing himself. 'Thanks, Maybie,' he said, taking some summer gel for himself. 'I know it's not gonna be fun, Peggro, but we can do this.' Then his stomach rumbled.

Phee let Russog down for a moment and took a stale bread roll from her bag, tearing it into five pieces and handing everyone a morsel.

Russog swallowed his whole, then sat at her feet, wagging his tail and licking his snout expectantly.

'Sorry, Stinkbomb,' she said, putting him back into the top of her backpack. 'We're gonna have to ration what's left for today.' She tied a white handkerchief over his head for a sunshade. They heard a high-pitched buzzing sound – Maybie's wings. She reappeared, shrunk down in her miniature dress, with Lulie Bean fluttering by her side.

Jayben carried her bag. 'Let's go!' he said, finishing his crust of bread, and they set off, trekking across the dry, dusty sand.

To keep their spirits up, they discussed what life might be like after Jayben defeated Null, when their families could be free, wondering what amazing objects Jayben might Free-Dream from the Earth World.

'Maybe we *will* find our dad,' said Peggro dreamily.

'And mine,' said Phee.

'And you'll remember everything, Jay-Jay,' said Maybie. 'Oh, it will be magical!'

The morning was long and arduous. As the sun rose higher, a breeze blew across the barren land, but it was stifling, like the air from an oven. They were yet to reach the shelter. Everyone had stopped talking, to keep their mouths from drying out. Lulie Bean had exhausted herself doing somersaults in the sky and ended up taking a nap in the top pocket of Jayben's shirt.

Suddenly she bolted up, her tiny nose twitching. Her wings buzzed and then *ZIP!* she soared into the air, turned right and whizzed off in a blur, disappearing over the top of a dune.

Jayben was baffled. 'I thought she was tired?' he said. 'Where's she going?'

Maybie shrugged, her wings slowing with exhaustion. 'She must have smelled something interesting.'

Jayben remembered when he'd first met the mee-mow, Maybie had told him that Lulie Bean couldn't resist candy and could smell it a mile away. 'Sweets?' he said.

'What are you talking about?' Peggro huffed, struggling to put one foot in front of the other, his sandals sticking to the hot sand. 'Why would there be candy in the desert? She's obviously gone mad with heatstroke.'

Jayben was intrigued and followed the direction Lulie Bean had taken. He slowly climbed to the top of the dune and gasped.

On the other side was a cluster of trees, shading a patch of grass and what looked like a pool of—

'WATER!' he croaked, and he hurried down.

'So we've all gone mad,' Peggro sighed, following him over the top. 'I told you we would. It's not real,

Jayben. This happens in the desert; it's called a mirage. You're hallucinating.'

But Jayben could still see the trees as he approached. They had straight green trunks and their twirly branches sparkled with tiny golden nuts. 'Helicorn trees!' he said, laughing hysterically and hurrying closer. 'Are they real?'

Phee quickly followed. 'It's really there, Peggro. I can see it too!'

'Of course you can,' he said, tutting behind them. 'That's how mass hallucinations work.'

Jayben was almost there, skidding down the dune. He spotted a picnic blanket on the grass under the trees, on which Lulie Bean was now happily sitting, nibbling on something tiny and red. He noticed there was someone sitting behind her, an old man with a long white beard and rosy cheeks, wearing a cream sunhat and a matching cream linen shirt and trousers.

Jayben called out to him. 'Hello?'

The old man looked up. 'Good grief, boy! I was wondering where this little creature had sprung from. Come into the shade!'

'Thank you,' Jayben whispered, too exhausted to wonder what an old man was doing out here in the desert, apparently having a picnic. He staggered under the shelter of the trees. The relief was overwhelming. He dropped to his knees and crawled across the grass to the water, plunging his hot, dusty face into it without hesitation. It was blissfully cool and he could taste its freshness. He resurfaced, laughing and cupping his hands for a drink.

'Guys! Come quick!' He laughed again. 'It's amazing!'

Phee rushed to join him, plunging into the pool, and she laughed even louder, drenching her hair.

'It's real?' Peggro gasped, dropping his satchel and appearing between them to dunk his face without even removing his glasses. As he came up for air, his glasses were still so hot they were giving off steam. 'Who cares whether it's real or not! It's wonderful!' He frowned. 'I just hope it's safe to drink.'

The old man chuckled. He was resting on a wooden cane. 'Safest water there is,' he said. 'A spring from deep underground. Only a few of these in the whole desert.'

'It's so cool!' said Jayben, throwing off his sandals to dunk his feet.

Phee laughed. 'I think that's the only time I've ever heard you use that word correctly.'

Maybie hovered at the edge, hesitating. 'Everyone

close your eyes, please,' she said, untying her bigger dress to empty her regular-sized shoes and hairband on to the grass.

Everyone looked away.

POOF!

The bright flash of white light. 'All done!' she said.

They turned around and there she was, back to the size of an average eight-year-old, straightening her yellow dress.

'Oinff! Oinff! Oinff!' Russog said, wriggling to escape Phee's backpack.

'Oh, sorry, Stinkbomb!' said Phee, removing his handkerchief.

Jayben noticed a sign beside the pool.

No Bathing!
Especially not animals

Too late.

'BATH TIME!' said Russog in Larnie's voice, before diving into the pool with a big splash, gleefully soaking his dirty green fur and blowing bubbles with his snout.

Jayben grinned. He realised then that in all the excitement they hadn't even asked the man's name.

'It's nice to meet you,' he said, holding his hand out. 'I'm Jayben.'

The man, who had been cheerfully holding his own hand out, froze, his eyes fixed on Jayben in disbelief. His gaze went to Jayben's open hand, the wet Rainbow crystals sparkling in his eyes. His jaw dropped.

'I don't believe it,' he whispered. Then he cheered. 'Jayben!' I never thought this day would come, but it has! I have finally found you!' He took his hand and shook it merrily. 'Or, rather, you found me.'

Found me? thought Jayben, thoroughly puzzled. 'Who – who are you?'

'Ah, let me introduce myself properly. It's just so wonderful! As I said, I was beginning to lose hope this day would come, after so long searching – why, I'm Mandon. Your grandpa.'

'*Grandpa Mandon?*' Jayben exclaimed. 'Peggro, we found him! We found our grandpa!'

Peggro leapt up and the two embraced. Jayben was overjoyed to find another member of his family, another piece of the puzzle. He noticed that Mandon wore a square blue charm around his neck. He was Trollwood, then, like Jayben's mother.

'But this is amazing!' Jayben cried. 'I have so many questions about our family. Like – like . . .' He felt so overwhelmed he didn't know where to start and ended up with, 'What was our mother like?'

'Yes!' said Peggro, shaking the water out of his hair. 'What *was* she like? Dad could never talk much about her or our life before he took me away to Bramalan seven years ago, and I was too young to remember her. I didn't even know I had a big brother – Jayben. Not until we found our grandma, Dad's mum. She explained what happened, the night our mother died, falling into the frozen lake in the woods, the night Jayben went to sleep for years. I can't believe we've found you!'

'Look,' said Jayben pulling his compass out of his pocket and opening it. He was shaking with excitement. 'My parents left me this.'

Mandon examined it and his eyes filled with tears. '*As long as you have a home to find you will never be lost.* Oh, my dear boys – I am so happy to have found you both.'

'Phee, Maybie!' Jayben cried, noticing they were hanging back, watching the reunion. 'This is my – my grandpa. Grandpa, these are our friends.' He felt proud and a bit shy. He wasn't used to introducing friends to family.

'Mee-mow!' said Lulie Bean, buzzing over to Mandon and hovering by his pocket.

Mandon chuckled, taking out a small paper bag. 'You *do* have a sweet tooth.' He emptied the bag into his palm – little red sweets, like the ones in Maybie's kitchen.

'So that's what she smelled,' said Jayben, as Lulie Bean swiped one of the candies and flew back to the picnic rug with it. 'We wondered why she zoomed off.'

'Plenty to go round,' said Mandon, before counting out the remaining sweets. 'One . . . two . . . three . . . four . . . five . . . six . . . seven . . . oh, goodness, not *that* one.' He stopped, picking out the eighth sweet and tossing it into the grass.

Jayben was baffled. 'What's wrong with that one?'

'Hmm?' said Mandon, like it was normal. 'Why, that was number eight! We couldn't eat that.'

Peggro whispered in his brother's ear. 'Superstition,' he explained. 'Some people avoid certain numbers, believing them to be unlucky.' He tutted disapprovingly. 'No science to it at all.'

Mandon smiled warmly, handing them each a sweet, including Russog.

'So,' said Mandon, taking one for himself, 'what in Sojan's name are you all doing out here in the desert?'

'I was going to ask you the same question,' said Jayben. 'The truth is, we—' He broke off as he noticed something behind his grandpa. On top of a picnic basket there was an open brown suitcase full of pieces of paper, flapping about in the breeze – just like he'd seen in his dream.

He gasped. *'The missing pages!'*

CHAPTER 18

Welcome to Karassan

Jayben ran to the suitcase, his hopes building. Could these really be the missing pages from the ancient *Book of Dreamers*?

'The missing pages?' asked Mandon, looking confused.

'Yes!' said Jayben, carefully picking up the top sheet of paper. 'I saw them in my dream, fluttering in a suitcase. Exactly like this. The Moonmother was showing me them for a reason – I just need to find the right words . . .'

He looked at the page, and to his surprise it was nothing like *The Book of Dreamers*. Strangely, almost every other word was in capital letters. He read it aloud:

The Chordian Guard

CLASSIFIED

A message from the chief's DAUGHTER:

Two of our guards IN the jungle, hunting for the witch in DISGUISE, had their JOURNEYS disrupted by a sea monster. They retreated TO avoid watery GRAVES. Now a fresh sighting OF the witch is reported at the GOLDEN cliffs - details in the GLASS bottle. The guards will resume their mission WHEN the MOON is full. They will meet the wizard where the sea BLOCKS the caves the next DAY. To STOP the witch, HER powers must be disabled. For the right price, the wizard AT the caves will rid her of ALL magic. They will advise the COST in due course.

Mandon pulled some other papers from his suitcase. 'Never mind that,' he said fiddling with his beard as if slightly nervous. 'I've got some great drawings to show you.'

'But, Grandpa,' said Jayben, pointing to the message. 'The witch? Do they mean Snaggis? Null's accomplice?'

He nodded, looking glum. 'I'm afraid she's still at large, wreaking havoc. She must be caught before—'

'So it's just a message?' Jayben blinked. He had been so sure these pages were important. Why else would the Moonmother have shown him them in his dream? 'But wait! Why are *you* getting messages from the Guard?'

Mandon laughed awkwardly, taking hold of the sheet. 'Because I'm *in* the Guard, dear boy.'

'Really?' said Jayben, eyes wide. 'My grandpa, in the Chordian Guard?'

Phee peered at the message. 'Why are some of the words in capital letters?' she asked.

'It's a code!' said Peggro excitedly. 'Old wizardish!'

'Oh, goodie!' said Maybie. 'Let's solve it!'

'Yes,' said Peggro, his finger to his chin, 'So the first word in caps is DAUGHTER . . .'

Mandon chuckled, folding it away. 'I should get you into the Guard, dear boy!' Then his face turned solemn. 'Or perhaps not. In fact, I don't think the Guard would approve of you seeing this at all. It's not information for children – not in these dark times. I could get into trouble.' He looked gloomy. 'There are things you're much better off not knowing.'

Jayben shook his head. 'But we know one of the Guards – she's called Raynor.'

Mandon frowned and then nodded. 'I've heard of her. An up-and-coming talent, I believe. So, she's been protecting you?'

'Yes! And I just fought Zamar, Grandpa. There's nothing I can't handle.' He turned back to the suitcase. 'I'm sure the Moonmother showed me these for a reason. The missing pages with the skeleton key words must be in here *somewhere*!'

Mandon shrugged. 'You're welcome to look, dear boy, and see if anything catches your eye. It's only what I have gathered on my journeys. I'm afraid it's rather a mess – I'm not terribly organised.'

Jayben rifled through the suitcase and found a roughly drawn map of the desert, a receipt from a hotel in Karassan and a list of poisonous plants to avoid in the Fairywood. There was nothing that looked remotely like it belonged in *The Book of Dreamers*.

He slumped to the ground in frustration. 'I don't get it,' he said with a heavy sigh. 'I definitely saw this in a dream. A suitcase like this, full of papers, under a tree in the desert. Why would the Moonmother show me that if they're not the missing pages?'

'Perhaps this isn't the right suitcase,' said Maybie, 'and you'll find the right one somewhere else.'

Peggro rolled his eyes. 'Or maybe it's as pointless as those arches you used to see in your dreams, Jayben, and we'll never know why you were seeing them.'

Phee playfully socked Peggro on the shoulder. 'Or maybe, Ben, she just wanted you to meet your grandpa?'

Jayben smiled. Phee had a point. As much as he'd have liked to have found the missing pages here, he was very glad to have found Mandon. He stood and shuffled the papers back together. 'I'm sorry,' he said. 'I just thought . . .'

'Don't be daft, boy,' said Mandon, smiling warmly. 'We're family. Besides, you have a good reason to want to find those pages. Dreams are not to be ignored. How magical it must be to see things in your sleep.'

'Thanks.' Jayben grinned, 'So is there any new information you *can* share with me? We got separated from Raynor. She's at sea.'

Mandon shook his head. 'I wish I did,' he said. 'But I haven't had any messages from Raynor or heard anything about you at all. There are strict rules about who is told what. It's all very need-to-know in the

Guard. The network of Jarmasters insist that any information they provide must be handled with care. They don't share memories from people's jars lightly.'

'Yes,' said Jayben. 'I remember our local Jarmaster telling me that.'

Mandon nodded. 'The Guard are right to be cautious. Those airtight rules are what's kept you safe since you went into hiding. Whoever your local Jarmaster is, they certainly can be trusted. Hasn't been so much as a whisper as to your whereabouts. Believe me, I've tried to find out since I heard you'd woken up and vanished from your grandma's house over a year ago.'

Jayben sighed. 'Well, *someone* must have figured out where I was. They broke into where I was sleeping and took the Golden Torch from me. Zamar was going to give it to Null, but we got it back.'

'Good grief!' said Mandon. 'Thank goodness. But how did you track Zamar down?'

'*He* came to *me*,' said Jayben. 'Zamar wanted to capture me.'

'Big mistake,' said Phee.

'Outstanding!' said Mandon, his eyes shining. 'When I heard that you, my grandson, had become a Dreamer – *the Final Dreamer* – and had so bravely

risen to the challenge, to fix the Torch at last, I couldn't have been more proud!'

'Well,' said Jayben, putting his arms around Peggro, Phee and Maybie. 'I couldn't do any of it without my friends. I know I'm the Dreamer but we've done everything as a team. I literally wouldn't be here without them. The four of us did it together.'

'Oinff!' said Russog, then in Jayben's voice he said, 'The five of us!'

Jayben laughed. 'The five of us!' Then a nasty thought occurred to him. 'Grandpa, you don't think . . . What if whoever told Zamar I had the Torch was someone in the Guard?' He turned to his friends. 'Raynor did warn us that the Observatory, the Guard's headquarters, had been compromised, remember?'

'That's how Null's Agents first got hold of those purple chordical glasses,' Phee said, looking worried. 'The ones they've been using to find Ben and the Torch. Raynor said she'd been very selective about who she told about his whereabouts, but she did communicate with some of her fellow Guards.'

Mandon tutted, shaking his head. 'Dear, dear, dear. If we, the Guard, can't be trusted, that's very worrying indeed. Thank goodness you've got the Torch back and that you're safe. That's all that matters now.'

Jayben proudly took out the Torch to show his grandpa.

Mandon's eyes lit up, reaching out to touch it. 'Extraordinary,' he whispered. 'And it's yours to carry now. My grandson.' He beamed.

Jayben put it away again and his grandpa composed himself. He closed the suitcase, fastening it with a padlock. 'We need to get you and the Torch out of this heat. I know a place in Karassan where we can rest until sunset.'

'Karassan?' said Jayben, taking the map out. 'But that's back in the Fairywood. In the wrong direction! If I'm going to stop Null then I need to be at that tomb before noon tomorrow. We have to keep going.'

'Goodness,' said Mandon, fiddling with his beard again. 'Null's going to a tomb? Whatever for?' Before they could answer, he swept on. 'We can't go further into the desert right now; it's too hot in the middle of the day. You'll die! And no beast would take you that far in this heat. We need to hurry to Karassan before it's too hot to move from here.'

Jayben stared around at the searing desert surrounding them. His grandpa was right – they couldn't continue in this heat. He met Phee's eyes and saw his own frustration reflected there.

'The city's not far,' Mandon continued. 'Just south of here. We'll be there before lunchtime.'

'But what about the nullheads there?' said Maybie. 'Aren't you worried about hearing the whispers? The curse?'

Mandon tapped his top pocket. 'Got my earplugs. We can rest and eat there and after sundown we can ride all night to that tomb, if it's so important. You can rest on the ride to the hotel.'

'Ride?' said Phee.

Mandon grinned at her, then called, 'Ready to go, Milro?'

They looked at each other, bewildered, for there was no one else there. Then, from behind one of the broad tree trunks, a shiny silver dome appeared, which seemed to be hovering a few feet above the ground. It was very large, the size of a carriage, and so shiny that Jayben could see their distorted reflection in the dome.

As they watched, from under the dome came a face, covered in scaly silver skin, on the end of a long wrinkly neck. It had big black eyes and a beak-like mouth. *A giant tortoise?* wondered Jayben, unsure how he knew what a tortoise was. He could see four legs moving under the dome as it slowly approached.

'Is that a momple?' asked Peggro.

'Indeed it is, my clever grandson,' said Mandon. 'A mirrorback momple to be precise. Her name is Milro.'

'Hi, Milro,' said Maybie, stroking the creature's face and feeding it a clump of grass.

'I've heard so much about these,' said Phee excitedly. 'In Fellooz, people ride them like trox.'

'Yup,' said Maybie. 'The best way to get around – if you don't have wings, of course.'

Mandon took the picnic rug off the grass and threw it over Milro's shell. Then he hooked his suitcase and picnic basket to a strap and took out a broad white parasol. 'Plenty of space for everyone,' he said, climbing on to the shell and opening the parasol, which shaded the entire rug.

Delighted not to be travelling on foot, Jayben gladly followed, sitting beside Mandon at the front. Phee, Peggro and Maybie squeezed on behind them, with Lulie Bean in Maybie's pocket and Russog on Phee's lap.

Mandon gave one of the reins to Jayben, then tapped Milro's shell and the mirrorback momple turned and began plodding away from the trees and into the blazing sun.

As the creature picked up its pace, Jayben felt beads of sweat running down his neck. In spite of the parasol's shade, the air was unbearably hot. 'Will Milro be okay?' he asked. 'Carrying all of us, in the heat?'

Mandon pointed ahead. 'She knows it's not far. And the sun's rays bounce off her mirrorback shell. These momples have evolved to survive here.'

Jayben could hear the others chatting behind him.

'So the first word of the coded message was DAUGHTER,' said Peggro.

'Right,' Phee whispered, 'then the second was IN, I think?'

'Then JOURNEYS,' Maybie suggested. 'Or was there something before that?'

'No, that can't be right,' said Phee. 'There was something—'

'DISGUISE!' said Peggro. 'That was it. But what was next? Grandpa Mandon, could we please take another look?'

Mandon chuckled. 'You *are* persistent, aren't you? Try to get some rest.'

Peggro whispered to Phee, 'We'll crack it.'

Ahead of them, Jayben could see the giant cacti of

the Fairywood again, but here they were even taller, with twice as many flowers. He noticed a broad gateway at the forest limits, an arch decorated with hundreds of tiny, coloured tiles – a mosaic of deep blues and vibrant oranges, and every shade in between. The dazzling design felt oddly familiar, like he had once drawn something similar, perhaps back in the Earth World.

Milro carried them under the arch, past a sign:

Welcome to Karassan
Adjust dials to FST

Jayben was intrigued. 'What's FST?' he asked.

'Fairywood Some Time,' Mandon explained, taking a small round bronze device from his pocket, about the size of Peggro's moondial. 'It's the time zone here – but everything revolves around mealtimes, and everyone eats at different times, so nobody's quite in sync.' He clicked a button and the sundial flipped over to simply display a question mark. 'See? Even the sundial doesn't know what time it is!'

Peggro shook his head disapprovingly. 'I still don't know how anything can function on Some Time. It must be chaos!'

Mandon slipped his dial back in his pocket. 'I make it about half past breakfast,' he said.

Russog's stomach rumbled loudly.

Mandon chuckled. 'Or perhaps it's more like quarter to lunch, where you're sitting.'

Milro walked on down a long dusty road cutting through the forest.

Jayben was puzzled to see no houses of any kind. Where did all the Fairywood people live? They turned left and soon found themselves at the top of a steep road, winding down the side of a canyon, to a vast city of white buildings with red-tiled roofs, sprawling up the banks of a narrow river.

Milro carried them down the road and then on to the first cobbled street of houses. There was no sign of any people, no sound over the hissing from the lush gardens of colourful flowering cacti.

'Maybe I should shrink down again,' Maybie said, looking around uneasily. 'I haven't been back to Karassan since those kids were taken. We shouldn't be out here in the street.' She took her golden charm off her neck to hide it in her pocket.

'It'll be all right,' said Mandon, putting his earplugs in. 'Everyone will be indoors with the sun this high. And besides, you're with me!' He pulled the reins to turn Milro on to a street of taller white buildings and then into a square of little shops and cafes, with a trickling fountain at its centre. 'No need to worry so much.'

But Jayben was struggling to control his nerves too. 'What if someone has those lenses? They could see my light through the windows.'

'Don't exhaust yourself fretting,' said Mandon firmly. 'I'm one of the Guard, remember? You're safe with me.'

Jayben nodded uncertainly. Something caught his eye, to the side of the square; something behind glass with a neatly printed sign beside it. Jayben was sure he'd seen a sign like that before. It read:

PROPERTY OF THE CROWN
Thieves will be <u>imprisoned</u>

Behind the glass, there was something familiar. A bright-red phone box, just like the one he had Free-Dreamed in the Giantwood. He felt as though it was jogging another memory too, but it remained out of reach. He frowned, looking past it to the bench beside the fountain.

'We'll be just fine,' said Mandon, his arm on

Jayben's shoulder, 'so long as we lie low and don't do anything to draw attention—'

CRACK!

In a bright flash of light the bench turned into a huge yellow digger.

CHAPTER 19

Lost in the Marble Market

'Ah,' said Mandon. 'I wasn't expecting *that*.'

Jayben gasped. 'I didn't mean to Free-Dream!' he said, looking nervously at the shop windows. The 'closed' sign of a coffee shop twitched, then the door of a bookshop opened.

'What the dune-hoppers is that?' said a woman, poking her head out to see the digger.

'Oh dear,' said Mandon, giving Milro a tap. 'So much for not attracting attention. Shall we, er, pick up the pace a bit?'

Milro trotted down an alley into a busy covered market with marble pillars, heaving with Karassanians, buying everything from fresh fruit to fabrics.

Mandon closed the parasol and slid down to tie the momple to a post by a shaded trough of water. 'Good girl. We'll come back for you,' he said, patting her on the head.

'Why are we stopping *here*?' asked Jayben, climbing down behind him. 'There are so many people!'

'Precisely,' said Mandon cheerfully, hobbling with his cane. 'Hard to see a needle amongst the cacti, as they say.'

'But . . .' Jayben paused. He was suddenly aware of a familiar and unpleasant feeling – a tingling in his left arm. It sometimes happened before a seizure. *Not again, not now*, he thought desperately.

Phee jumped down beside him. 'You okay, Ben?' she asked.

Jayben saw the alley over her shoulder. The woman from the bookshop and a few others who'd seen the digger were following them curiously. Jayben had to disappear. No time to worry about his head.

'I'm fine,' he said, trying for a smile. 'Let's go.'

Phee didn't look convinced, but there was no time to lose. Mandon led them into the busy market, past a large sign which read:

HIGH RISK
(OF WHISPERS)
EARPLUGS MUST BE WORN
AT ALL TIMES

Russog leapt into Phee's backpack and everyone hurried into the bustling market, squeezing between shoppers and their loaded baskets, as the traders shouted out their offers from all sides.

'Fine spices!' a man bellowed to Jayben's right, thumping a sack against a weighing scale. 'Get your fine spices!'

A woman to his left clapped a pair of shoes together and yelled, 'Half-price sandals!' She thrust them at Jayben. 'How many marbles you got, son?'

He said nothing and kept shuffling forward. He could barely make sense of what they were saying over all the noise from every stand in the market. The chopping of a butcher's knife, the jingling of windchimes, the sizzling of a frying pan and the clinking of china cups, all combined with the murmuring shoppers, stabbing in his brain. Even the smells were overwhelming. Pungent cheeses, overripe fruit and the pong of leather goods in the warm, musty air. It didn't seem to be bothering anybody else, though.

This is what happens, Jayben thought, *before a seizure*. Sounds grew too loud, lights too bright, smells too strong. His brain was sounding the alarm once again. His heart raced, he felt dizzy and he stopped, closing his eyes, trying to take deep breaths. *It's going to be okay*, he thought to himself, desperately trying to calm his nerves. *So long as I'm not alone*. Someone jostled him and he opened his eyes to realise he couldn't see his friends.

'Guys?' he called out, frantically looking in all directions. He'd reached the centre of the market, where several aisles met under the many marble pillars. *Which one had they taken?* His head spun and the colours, smells and sounds began to blur—

Then he heard a gentle voice from behind. 'You poor child. Are you all right?'

He turned to see a woman about his grandma's age, with pale cheeks, twinkly blue eyes and silver waves under her lavender headscarf. She held out her hand with a smile. 'You mustn't be so sad.'

There's something calming about her, he thought.

'What's your name, dear?' she asked, removing her earplugs.

He couldn't tell her. It wasn't safe. He quickly thought of Phee's cousin. 'Nilthan,' he replied. 'I – I need to find my friends. They were just here. But now they're gone.'

She gently stroked his cheek, wiping away his tears. Her hands were as soft as silk. 'Lost in the marble market – how dreadful,' she said. 'All this noise and the smells. It's too much for your poor head.'

'How do you know about my head?' Jayben asked, wiping his eyes with a sniff.

'It's my gift, dear,' she said, pointing to a pendant around her neck, a clear crystal ball. 'I know exactly what is wrong and I can help you. Here.' From her headscarf she took a small white flower and gave it to him. 'Smell this.'

Intrigued, he took a sniff and it was like he was back in the Giantwood – the sweet aroma of sap in the fresh forest air, peppered with the scent of woodsmoke. It smelled like . . . home. And to his astonishment, the noises seemed to soften, and the smells no longer bothered him. His head felt instantly better.

'What is this?' he said.

She smiled. 'An old sort of magic. Come,' she said, gesturing to one of the aisles. 'I'll help you find your loved ones.'

Jayben paused for a moment. He was supposed to

be lying low, not accepting help from strangers. But there was still no sign of the others in the sea of chaos, and he didn't feel safe standing here, exposed and alone. Whoever this woman was, she had soothed his head and made him feel less vulnerable. He couldn't help wanting to go with her, so he did.

'What's your name?' he asked, following her down one aisle, past a counter where people exchanged lengths of gold ribbon for handfuls of glass marbles.

'Terrisell, dear. I'm so glad we've met.' She stopped by a blue velvet curtain, closed around a stall, and drew it open slightly. 'Here we are.'

Jayben took another sniff of the flower and gladly walked through, to find himself in a trove of treasures. There were cabinets dripping with jewellery, boxes overflowing with ornaments and in the middle of a table, on a dark purple cloth, sat a large crystal ball.

'Come, sit,' she said, pulling a stool from under the table.

He sat by the crystal ball while Terrisell rummaged in a cupboard. 'Ah! Here it is,' she said, holding a short, straight stick with a few tiny holes at one end. 'Now, let's see.' She took a jar of cut red flowers from a shelf and placed them by the crystal ball. Then she pulled a tiny bottle from her pocket, removing the cork to take a sniff. Her eyes widened, she waved the stick at the flowers and said the words 'Craino. Fraino. Shtoom!'

POOF!

There was a bright flash and Jayben jumped. The flowers in the jar were now white and he could smell the forest again and the sweet scent of the Fellers' house.

A magic wand? he wondered, having heard a lot about them from Maybie. Was she a witch, or a Fairywood with old magic? He couldn't see a clanband charm on her.

'How did you do that?' he asked.

Terrisell simply smiled and handed him the jar. 'For you, sweet child.'

'Really?' he said, his head feeling calmer still. Whatever was in these flowers they were doing a much better job than the tonic. He felt warm inside, imagining never having to worry about seizures again. 'Thank you,' he said, burying his nose in the petals. 'How much are they? I don't have any money on me right now, but—'

'No, no, no,' said Terrisell with a chuckle. 'I couldn't take payment. I just wish I had the power in this wand to heal you for good.'

'For good?'

She nodded. 'The flowers can only offer relief for a time. They'll be dead by tomorrow.'

Jayben sighed. He should have known it was too good to be true. Still, at least he was safe for today.

The woman added, 'I know a spell that would do it, though.' She turned to put the wand back on a shelf. 'If only I had the strength of a crystal wand.'

With Terrisell's back turned, Jayben opened his palm to look at his Rainbow crystals and the darker crystals he'd taken from Null. He knew they were incredibly powerful. *What if she can really heal me?* he thought. He'd still have more crystals than Null – and he'd be spared the risk of having a seizure tomorrow at the tomb.

When he got home to Ampelwed he'd have the right medicine again, but until then he was in constant danger. This woman, Terrisell, could help. Surely he could trust her?

He made his mind up and turned his hand to show his crystals. 'Would these work?' he said.

Terrisell's eyes widened and she let out a gasp, clutching her pendant. 'Rainbow crystals! The most powerful in all the world,' she whispered.

Jayben smiled nervously. 'Would a few of these be

enough for you to make your wand strong? Strong enough to make my head better? For ever?'

'Dear child,' she said, eagerly fetching the wand, 'with Rainbow crystals, there's little a wand can't do. Now, just hold out your hand . . .'

CHAPTER 20

A Wand for a Pencil

Jayben held out his palm, his heart beating fast. *This could be it.* A life without seizures, a life where he kept his memories . . .

Terrisell began waving the wand over the crystals, back and forth, then whispered a spell. 'Bom. Pah. Do. Beetum. Bom. Pah. Do. Beetum.' She repeated the words. 'Bom. Pah. Do. Beetum.'

Jayben waited. Nothing was happening.

Maybe she's made a mistake, he thought. *Is it too good to be true?*

But then all of a sudden he felt pressure in his hand, then he felt dizzy.

'Bom. Pah. Do. Beetum. Bom. Pah. Do. Beetum.'

 227

POP! POP! POP!

Sparks flew between them and not one, not two, but every single one of the darker crystals broke away to be sucked into the holes of the wand, leaving only Jayben's original ones in his hand.

Terrisell's face lit up. 'It worked!' she said, raising her wand, the embedded crystals glowing.

Jayben felt weak and cold, slumping on the stool. 'That's too many!' he cried out.

Terrisell didn't reply, staring at her glimmering wand.

'Well?' he said. 'Are my seizures gone for good?'

To his surprise Terrisell broke into a laugh, then scurried back to the cupboard, pulling out a green gown.

He noticed a bracelet under her sleeve with a silver star-shaped charm. *Spritewood*. Like the witch Snaggis, Null's accomplice.

A cold feeling settled over him. *Was Terrisell a northern witch?*

'My dear child,' she said, putting a few things in a bag. 'I confess, there is no such spell.'

'What?' he cried. He tried to stand, but he was too weak. 'What do you mean?'

She held up the glowing wand with a grin, and he

could see every fault in the dark Rainbow crystals, tightly locked between the twisted lines in the wood.

'Thank you for the crystals, Dreamer.' Then she held out something else, tauntingly. A purple lens.

It had all been a dirty trick. She had seen him coming.

He stood up, seething with anger, still dizzy. 'You lied to me!' he said. 'Give me those crystals back! I – I'll get my friends, they'll stop you!'

'I'm afraid you're not going anywhere,' Terrisell said, buttoning her bag. She waved the wand at him. 'Espadol . . .'

Frantically, he tried to use his Trollwood magic to seize her wand, but it didn't budge. It was as if losing those crystals had affected his old magic. He felt helpless – and it struck a chord inside. The unfairness. The cruelty. Having his things stolen and feeling utterly *powerless*.

It felt like a memory. Of being locked in an empty classroom.

'. . . Orpadol . . .' she continued.

The wand started shaking and glowing as an image popped into his mind—

CRACK!

A bright flash and the wand was turned into a pencil.

Terrisell dropped it, trembling, looking as if she'd been wounded. 'NO!' she cried.

Jayben was shocked. Where in the Earth World had he sent those crystals, and how could he get them back? Then he heard a familiar noise.

'Oinff! Oinff! Oinff!' Russog came bounding through the curtain, his curly tail wagging.

Terrisell looked furious, dropping her green gown. 'This will cost you,' she said menacingly.

'It already has!' said Jayben, as Russog sat at his feet. The noises and smells started to bother him again. He stumbled to his knees, reaching for the flowers, but they'd already shrivelled, and the sweet smell was gone.

He saw Terrisell taking something from the cabinet – a silver dagger. She turned, pointing it at Jayben. He flinched – when suddenly the dagger flew backwards, out of her hand, smashing into the cabinet. The curtain was thrown open and in stepped Mandon, his Trollwood charm glowing.

'Get away from my grandson!' he snapped, standing between them. 'Spritewood menace!' He lifted both arms and the cabinet flipped up, spilling Terrisell's treasures everywhere.

'Ben!' said Phee, rushing to help him up. 'We were so worried!'

Terrisell backed into the corner. 'You Trollwoods are all the same.'

Mandon picked up the jar of wilted flowers. 'You tried to poison him?' He threw the jar at the cupboard and it shattered against the jewellery.

Terrisell shuffled back, cowering.

Jayben was shocked. It was the first time he'd had a family member defend him like this. Relieved as he was to see Mandon and his friends, he was riddled with guilt for trusting a total stranger, costing him so much of his power, all because he couldn't wait a few days to get his medicine back.

Mandon shouted at Terrisell. 'Where is it? 'Your wand?' He tipped up the table and her crystal ball fell, cracking in two.

Jayben bent down and picked up the plain beige pencil, filled with regret. 'It's gone,' he said. He didn't tell them about the crystals – he couldn't quite bear to. 'I sent it to the Earth World. A wand for a pencil.'

Mandon nodded. 'Good lad.' He picked up Terrisell's green gown and the purple lenses. 'Don't ever come near him again,' he warned her, putting his arm around Jayben. And with that, they walked away, closing the curtain on Terrisell and her broken crystal ball.

CHAPTER 21

Three Quiet Diners

In the midday sun, the cobbles of Karassan city felt like hot coals under Jayben's sandals. His grandpa chattered away, explaining that they had tied the momple in the shade, to rest for the night's journey, and that they were walking to a hotel. Everything ached. But he barely noticed the discomfort with so much weighing on his mind. With every step he felt more regret. How could he have been so foolish as to have been conned out of so many Rainbow crystals, the day before he would need them most?

'I'm so sorry,' he said, as they wandered into a shaded alley of blooming vines. 'For getting lost in the market. I'm sorry for everything.'

'What are you talking about?' said Phee, putting her arm around him. 'You've got nothing to apologise for.'

He stopped for a moment. Noises from the shuttered windows were bothering him. Cutlery scraping crockery inside. People gossiping. Another skoggle barking somewhere.

'She tricked me,' he sighed. 'Terrisell told me she knew a spell that could fix my head and stop my seizures for good. To do it she needed a few crystals in her wand.' He held out his palm. 'But she took so many!'

'Oh dear,' said Mandon, seeing that the swirl of darker crystals had gone. 'Oh, that is unfortunate. But those witches can be terribly sneaky, dear boy.'

'How could I be so stupid?' Jayben cried, his eyes welling. 'I should have known it was too good to be true, but my head was scaring me. I thought I was going to have a seizure in the market – on my own. Then she gave me those flowers and I felt better. I wanted to believe she could fix me. So stupid!'

'You're not stupid at all!' said Phee angrily. '*She* is the stupid one! For underestimating *you*. What she did was evil, Ben. Exploiting a kid's illness, for moon's sake! And, honestly, I'd have done the same. If I had seizures like you, I'd do just about anything to feel better.' She squeezed Jayben's hand. 'But even with all her tricks – she still lost. Because you're good. You have friends. I know your seizures are horrible, but I don't ever want to hear you saying that you need fixing, Ben. You're the strongest, bravest, kindest person I know.'

Phee's words brought Jayben so many emotions. A wave of sadness for the illness he couldn't escape, but also a warm feeling of pride, because Phee was right – he *wasn't* weak or foolish and his illness *didn't* define him. Tears streamed down his cheeks.

She gave him a hug, then rubbed her knuckles over his head. 'Got it?'

It made him laugh. 'Thanks, Phee,' he said, wiping his eyes. 'You're right.'

Phee grinned. 'Always. Duh.'

Maybie hugged Jayben's side. 'You did a great job Free-Dreaming her wand away, Jay-Jay!' she said. 'Magical!'

'Yes,' Peggro agreed. 'You seem to be able to do it more now, when you need to.'

Jayben wasn't sure. Some of the Free-Dreaming had worked out – turning Zamar's flashpin into a washing machine that morning, and the wand into a pencil.

But he still felt out of control when it came to his powers. He couldn't decide what to Free-Dream – or when.

'I didn't mean to do that digger in the square earlier,' he said. 'That one didn't help us – it drew attention to us! And if I hadn't done it, we wouldn't have rushed into the market, and I wouldn't have ended up meeting Terrisell.'

'That was my fault,' said Mandon. 'I shouldn't have rushed you in such a busy place where we could get separated. From now on, we'll stick together.' He waved his glowing charm at Jayben. 'And, as it happens, that Free-Dream in the square seems to have restored my old magic!' He laughed, looking giddy. 'I could get used to this!' He pointed at a drain and from it a penny flew into his hand.

Jayben smiled. 'I'm glad you have it back, especially as I can't seem to use my Trollwood magic at the moment.' He looked at a pebble between two cobbles, trying to pull it. It wobbled but stayed on the ground. 'I think it's because I lost those crystals,' he sighed. 'Half of my power!'

'No,' said Peggro. 'They were *Null's* crystals – the ones you took from him. Who knows what harm they might have been doing you with his energy in them?

Now you're just back to how you were before, with the crystals you're meant to have. You did a lot with those last time, remember?'

'That's the spirit,' said Mandon.

Jayben nodded. 'True,' he said, feeling some confidence returning. His left arm was tingling, his brain was still sounding the alarm, but he was trying not to think about it. At least he was with people he could trust. Whether he liked it or not, he couldn't succeed ln life without help. But, outside of his circle of friends, who could he trust? After what happened with Terrisell just now, and how they'd been betrayed by Yespa a year ago, it was harder to answer that question.

Before he could give it another thought, his stomach rumbled.

Like clockwork, Phee's rumbled too.

'Aha!' said Mandon, taking out his pocket sundial and tapping on the question mark. 'I make that precisely lunch o'clock.'

Russog sang in Larnie's voice, '*Breakfaaast!*'

Everyone laughed and Mandon led them down another street. As they walked, Jayben admired the design of the houses and shops, each one decorated with a unique mosaic of colourful tiles. Everything seemed to have closed for the afternoon, but then Mandon spotted a small cafe where they weren't quite finished stacking the chairs away.

HooNo's
Longest Roll in Fellooz

'Ooooh!' said Maybie, licking her lips. 'I haven't had a HooNo's in for ever!'

Jayben was hit by the most mouth-watering smell of buttery pastry. It was tempting – but he was anxious to get to the hotel and out of sight.

'Is it safe to stop?' he asked.

'We can eat them on the go,' said Mandon. 'You must be famished.'

They peeked inside. The place was empty but for three quiet diners sitting in the window – young men dressed in white linen suits. Mandon handed Peggro Terrisell's rolled-up gown and purple monocle so he could get his purse of marbles out to pay. Peggro rolled up the gown and stashed it in his satchel.

'You wait here,' Mandon said, and went inside for a few moments, before returning with a foot-long roll of flaky pastry for each of them.

'What's inside?' asked Jayben, eyeing his.

'Nobody knows what's in a HooNo's,' said Phee with her mouth full. 'Just that it's *gooood*.'

It was true. After one bite of the cheesy, nutty, fruity local delicacy, Jayben felt a lot better.

'Not far to the hotel now,' said Mandon, passing a bottle of water through the door. But, as Mandon was paying, Jayben spotted something stitched into the white linen shirt of one of the quiet diners: nine grey squares, and the words: *Agents of the Ninth*.

The man looked directly at him. Trying to keep his expression calm, Jayben whispered to the others, 'We need to go.'

Mandon hurried out. The Agent stood up, mouthing something to the other two, before holding a purple-tinted glass to his eye.

Jayben's heart jumped. 'Run!' he cried, as the men reached for their holsters.

Everyone ran down the street, to a tiled bridge across the trickling river. Mandon was struggling to keep up, hobbling with his cane in the blistering heat. And then—

CHAPTER 22

Dragon Silk

Jayben felt a cold chill. He opened his eyes to see the desert in near darkness . . . through the bars of a cage that felt like it was moving.

Panicking, he tried to move his tingling arms but they were pinned behind his back with what felt like metal handcuffs. He looked around. The cage was covered on top. It was rocking and he could hear the plodding of momple feet in the sand. He looked to the other corners of the cage to see Phee, Peggro and Maybie all slumped, asleep, their hands tied to the bars behind their backs. Mandon was nowhere to be seen.

'Wake up!' he said, dreading to think what had happened.

'Hmm?' Phee moaned with a yawn. She looked up. 'Ben!' she cried, then lowered her voice to a whisper. 'How are you feeling?'

'Where are we?' he asked, tugging at the handcuffs, desperate to free his arms, but they were locked fast. 'What's happening?'

'It's okay,' she whispered. 'You need to stop that, or they'll hear us.'

'Who is *they*?' he asked, fearing the answer. In the dim light he could see two pairs of legs dangling from the roof at the front, and reins hanging between them, tied to a couple of momples.

'Agents,' she whispered. 'You had another seizure, last night – a big one, before they put us in here. You've probably forgotten a lot of yesterday.'

Yesterday? What time was it now? He looked ahead, through the bars. The horizon was beginning to glow pink.

'It's nearly dawn,' said Phee.

'How?' he said, trying to recall something – anything. He remembered the Agents in the cafe and running through the streets of Karassan and then – nothing. 'Where's Mandon? And Russog? And Lulie Bean?' His panic grew, looking at the blankets over their legs for any sign of a friendly green snout.

241

'It's okay,' said Phee again, with a sigh that told him that really nothing was okay. 'The Agents chased us to the river before they captured us – Mandon couldn't keep up. We lost him.'

Jayben hung his head. He'd only just found his grandpa and now he was lost again.

'Russog and Lulie Bean are up there,' she said, tilting her head up to the roof of the cage. 'In a basket.'

Jayben noticed something else – his right pocket felt lighter than usual. His heart sank. 'The Torch?'

Phee nodded grimly. 'One of Zamar's men took it. He left before they put us in here. They're taking us to Zamar's dungeon, in his palace.'

In his other pocket he could feel the cold smooth shape of his compass, the edges of the map and the jagged points of a rock against his leg. The star glass. That was something at least.

At that moment, Maybie gave out a yawn and blinked over at Jayben. 'Jay-Jay!' she said. 'You're awake! How's your head?'

'Huh?' said Peggro, jolting awake at the sound of her voice. He raised his head, his glasses crooked. 'Oh no,' he said, looking left and right, anxiously wriggling his legs under Terrisell's green gown. 'I hoped I'd imagined this! And why is this gown out of my bag? What else have they taken?'

Maybie smiled nervously at Jayben. 'Now that you're awake, it's all going to be okay.'

Phee nodded firmly. 'That's what I keep saying. We can figure a way out of this, right?'

Jayben said nothing, trying to think.

'Look,' said Peggro, staring through the bars to the west. 'The moon – and the sun!'

Jayben looked to see the moon rising on the horizon. Then he turned to the east, squinting in the golden sunrise. He remembered what the others had told him.

When the moon met the sun in the sky . . . *the eclipse*. He felt sick.

Peggro tugged at his restraints, looking worried. 'Just a few notches of a sundial and it'll be too late.'

'We can't give up—' began Jayben, before breaking off, staring at his brother. Peggro's Dragonwood charm was glowing and Jayben noticed that the green gown had vanished from his lap – along with, apparently, his brother's legs, clad in his shorts. As Jayben watched, Peggro's face and arms disappeared too, leaving just a shirt and a pair of glasses in mid-air.

'Peggro?' he said. 'Are you there?'

Peggro reappeared and so did the gown on his legs.

'That's weird,' said Phee slowly. 'Usually when Peggro turns invisible, all his clothes stay behind. But this time his shorts and the gown vanished too.'

'The witch's gown!' Peggro said excitedly. 'It must be made of dragon silk!' He turned to Jayben to explain. 'In the Magic Ages the dragon folk used to wear dragon silk because it would react when they went invisible – so their clothes didn't give them away. It vanishes along with you.'

'Magical!' said Maybie. 'Can you do it again, Peggro?'

He nodded and then, sure enough, he, his shorts and the gown disappeared again for a moment.

'Whoa!' said Phee. 'And you did it on purpose too! How did you manage that?'

For the first time Peggro didn't look unsettled by his magic. Instead, he looked very pleased with himself. 'I just – I just thought about being worried,' he said. 'Which wasn't hard, given the situation. And it worked!'

'That is so cool, Peggro,' said Jayben. He could feel his Trollwood charm pressing into his wrist. Maybe his old magic would work again now that some time had passed. Perhaps that could help them escape?

He noticed a loose screw on the cage floor by his foot. He fixed his gaze on it and thought about having it in his hand. It twitched slightly but it wouldn't move from its spot. With a huff of frustration, he gave up and started pulling at his handcuffs again.

He hated the feeling of being trapped. He hated the feeling of having things taken from him. That emotional chord deep inside felt like it was bringing back another memory. Of being locked in a bathroom as a punishment. It was getting clearer, and he realised that something was about to happen—

'A Free-Dream!' he said. 'Phee! Quick!'

If they were touching as he Free-Dreamed, her powers would also be restored. He stretched his leg as far as it would go in her direction, trying to touch her foot.

He could feel the memory. Something everyday, something white and slender, with bristles . . . It was almost there . . .

Phee stretched her sandal towards his, but there was still an inch between them.

Jayben could almost see something in his mind, see it taking shape . . .

With a groan, she strained and the tip of her big toe touched his.

The screw started to shake and glow.

CRACK!

In a flash of light, the screw turned into an electric toothbrush.

And from behind Phee's back came a red glow. Her Giantwood charm was shining.

CHAPTER 23

The Glass City

They all looked at each other, eyes wide. Jayben heard the Agents shuffling on the roof. Had they heard the noise or seen the flash from the Free-Dream?

Jayben kicked the toothbrush under his blanket, whispering to his friends. 'Pretend we're asleep.'

They all half closed their eyes, leaning back against the bars.

Jayben spied a man's face peeping down at them from the roof. After looking at each of them for a moment, he disappeared again.

'Coast's clear,' whispered Jayben.

There was a quiet snapping sound from the bars near Phee, and she brought her arms forward, holding a pair of broken handcuffs.

'I missed this!' she said, grinning and crawling over to Jayben to reach behind his back. 'Now we can bust out of here!'

Maybie beamed. 'Me next! I can't wait to free poor Russog and Lulie Bean!'

Peggro looked nervous, turning invisible again, his glasses hovering above his shirt. 'But they have flashpins,' he whispered, reappearing, 'and Phee lost her fishdart, remember?'

Phee snapped the restraints from everyone's wrists as if they were made of matchsticks. 'We have the element of surprise,' she said.

'Wait,' said Jayben. 'They're taking us to the dungeon, right – and the dungeon is *inside* Zamar's palace?'

Maybie nodded. 'One kid who escaped told us where they were kept, before they were put to work.'

'Amazing!' said Jayben. A plan started to form in his mind. 'What if . . .' he said, 'we *don't* bust out of here, not yet? They've taken the Torch again, back to Zamar, right? If we sit tight, then we'll be taken straight into his palace.'

'Right into his lair?' said Peggro with a shudder.

'I don't know about this, Jayben,' said Phee uneasily. 'If I can disarm the Agents now, we can steal the wagon and drive ourselves to the tomb, before the solar eclipse at noon.'

'But my powers are weak. Peggro, you said it yourself – and they all have flashpins. Without the Torch, how can I stop Null from entering the tomb? No. I need it – *before* we go to the tomb. The palace will be heavily guarded. But if we wait a bit longer and pretend we're still tied up, they'll take us straight through into the palace – the Torch.' He grinned. 'The element of surprise, like you said, Phee.'

Phee nodded, looking like she was weighing things in her mind. 'Raynor said the important thing was protecting the tomb,' she said slowly.

'And the palace is huge,' said Maybie. 'We don't know where the dungeon is and there will be lots of guards.'

'But far fewer than if we had to fight our way inside, right?'

'All right,' said Phee, sitting back down. 'To stop Null from entering the tomb, we need all the power we can get. We need the Torch. Let's go to Zamar's palace.'

Everyone sat back in their corners of the cage, arms behind their backs as though still cuffed. As the sun rose higher, the moon was steadily climbing the crystal-clear blue sky from the west. It was less visible now in the daylight, but it was there, on its way to crossing the sun's path at noon.

Peggro held the purple lens that Mandon had given him to his eye and squinted at the sun. 'Raynor said it's safe to look at through these. I can't believe we're actually going to see a total solar eclipse! It's fascinating. Even Grandma's only seen *one* in her lifetime, when she was young.'

'My dad always wanted to see an eclipse,' said Phee sadly. 'He'll miss it.'

Jayben tried not to think about Tedrik, and how unfair it was that he'd been nullheaded. He couldn't dwell on the sadness – he needed to focus on what lay ahead.

He tried to imagine the eclipse, the moon blocking the sun in the middle of the day. Awesome as it would be in normal times, he could only dread it. The ring of magical light it would give off, charging the star glass gems in the tomb, ready to make Null's Rainbow crystals three times more powerful. No, so far he was not an eclipse fan.

He picked up the toothbrush he had brought from the Earth World and grinned. Yesterday he'd sent half of Null's crystals to that world, in Terrisell's wand.

For now, Jayben was still the most powerful Dreamer. And it could stay that way – if he could just keep Null away from those yellow gems.

'Here we are,' Maybie whispered, pointing through the bars in the blinding daylight. 'The outskirts of the city of Zamar.'

They were approaching a few houses of some sort, little huts made of dry reeds, baked in the sun. Unlike Karassan, there were no flowers here – no plants of any kind. Instead, scattered around these small abodes were piles of scrap metal, wheelbarrows full of used tins and bottles, and sacks of old rags.

As they passed a house with a broken roof, Jayben caught sight of a gaunt young man inside, coughing uncontrollably as he tried to mend a shirt. He was deathly pale, with dark circles around his eyes.

In the next house he saw a woman who was practically skeletal, watching her small children draw pictures on the dusty floor with their fingers.

Jayben was shocked. He'd never seen such deprivation.

Phee looked just as disturbed. 'Why are they living like this?' she asked. 'Can't someone help?'

'It didn't used to be this way,' said Maybie sadly. 'These people used to live by the sea, in a coastal town, which is now Zamar's city. They weren't rich there but it was a good town. Then Null sent Zamar here, three years ago. The big baddie made a few local people very rich and they helped him change everything. They built the glass city on what used to be the old coastal town and everything just became too expensive for ordinary people – so they were pushed out of the city, to live in these slums on the outskirts.'

They passed a house where an old man was packing a bag beside a notice.

Eviction Notice
Due to failure to pay rent

Next door, there was an empty house missing a wall, with a different sign.

TO LET
24 marbles / day

Phee gasped. 'Twenty-four marbles a day? To live *there*? That's like two feet of gold ribbon! Why don't they just move to somewhere like Karassan?'

Maybie shook her head. 'This was their hometown. And Karassan isn't safe – neither is anywhere else in the Fairywood. The whispers. Everyone's scared to catch Null's curse. They're safe from that here, at least – Zamar's made it illegal to care for a nullhead, even if they're family. They're all sent to special places outside of town, in the desert, until they can be used for basic tasks in factories.'

'Special places?' asked Jayben with a shiver. They saw a man and a woman approaching the side of the plodding momples.

One of the Agents on the roof shouted, 'Get back!'

'Please,' the woman begged. 'We need to eat. Just one marble?'

'This is loaded,' said the Agent, presumably aiming his flashpin. 'Get back or I'll use it.'

Jayben pressed against the bars, watching their desperate faces as they passed by. He felt so helpless.

They turned on to a gravel road with an incline, travelling up past a few warehouses and slightly larger homes with the odd coloured tile for decoration. The road became steeper and then they stopped.

A group of armed Agents slowly opened an enormous gate; it was at least ten feet tall. The white stone wall either side of it was even higher.

With the crack of a whip, the momples walked through, into a lush green landscape of fountains, flower beds and sweet-smelling fruit trees.

Jayben saw a paved footpath leading to an enormous house made of glass, with golden balconies on multiple levels. It was one of dozens of similar properties, with lush gardens between them, leading to a procession of gigantic glass columns on either side of the road. They were at least a hundred feet tall, though it was hard to look at them due to the dazzling sparkles from inside. He squinted and could see that each column was crammed full of tiny glass balls. 'Are those *marbles*?' he asked.

Nobody answered. They were all stunned.

'But there must be thousands in there. Millions!' How could Zamar keep so much money locked in here when there was such dire poverty outside the gates?

Jayben heard the bars of the cage creaking, bending in Phee's clenched fists. She looked more furious with every pillar of wealth they passed in the glass city. 'Talk about filthy rich,' she muttered.

Suddenly blinding light shone into the cage. Jayben shielded his eyes and peered ahead. There it was. A colossal tower of glass, pointing into the sky, like a narrow pyramid, dwarfing even the columns. At its base there was a golden lift with a large letter 'Z' on its railings. It reached all the way to the top of the tower.

Zamar's palace.

And they were going right inside.

The Agents drove them down a ramp, passing a courtyard full of children in white gowns who were lining up in neat rows, facing the golden lift.

Maybie leapt up. 'Fairywoods!' she gasped. 'It's them! I can see their dots, where their wings used to be!'

Phee grabbed her hand. 'Shhh!' she said. 'The Agents will hear us, Maybie.'

'But – but –' she said. 'I could shrink down here and help them now. It's them, Phee! We found them!'

Jayben was desperate to free them, but it would have to wait. He put his arm around Maybie. 'We'll help them, Maybie. I promise. And you can shrink down soon. But right now, it's too risky. We have to deal with Zamar first. We need to get the Torch back. And then we need to get to the tomb.'

Peggro whispered from his corner of the cage, 'We're stopping! Sit back down. Quick!'

Everyone got back into their places, hands behind their backs, eyes closed.

The courtyard disappeared from view as the cage was driven inside, beneath the glass tower, then slowed to a stop.

Jayben opened one eye to see three Agents guarding the top of a flight of stairs. Above it was an arrow, pointing down, and the words:

TROUBLEMAKERS
CLIPPED FAIRYWOODS ONLY

Beside it there was a closed golden door, marked with a letter 'Z', just like the lift.

The two Agents on the roof of the cage stepped down, flashpins in their holsters.

Jayben took a deep breath and whispered to Phee, 'This is it.'

They were about to enter Zamar's palace.

CHAPTER 24

The Golden Doors

Phee subtly nodded at Jayben as one of the Agents took a key to open the cage door. Jayben nodded back and . . .

WHAM!

Phee kicked the door off its hinges like it was made of cardboard, sending it slamming into the Agent, knocking him to the floor. Leaping out, she grabbed the Agent next to him and threw him towards the staircase. He dropped his flashpin, which clattered down the stairs.

'That's for my dad!' she shouted, her nostrils flaring.

Two of the other Agents ran towards them.

Phee swung one of the bars and knocked them both out. 'That's for those Fairywood kids!'

Peggro and Maybie escaped the cage and ran to hide behind the momples.

Jayben darted to one of the unconscious Agents, snatching the keys from his hand.

The Agent by the stairs climbed to his feet, only for Phee to kick him in the chest, knocking him down again. 'And *that's* for my friends!' Her expression of triumph changed to one of alarm. 'Jayben – behind you!'

Jayben turned to see the last Agent standing by the door, aiming a flashpin right at him.

'No!' shouted Phee, running towards him. *She'll never make it in time*, Jayben thought desperately.

The Agent grinned, his finger tightening on the trigger – but, just as he fired, he stumbled, as though pushed from behind. The weapon shot into the ceiling and the Agent fell to the ground.

Peggro's face appeared by the door, peeking out of the dragon-silk gown.

'Nice one, little bro!' said Jayben, then he heard the buzz of wings. Maybie had shrunk down and was tugging at the basket on top of the cage. 'A little help with this?'

Jayben hurried over and grabbed the basket. Russog and Lulie Bean were sound asleep inside, oblivious to the drama. 'Let's go!' he said, as Phee grabbed her backpack and chucked Peggro his satchel.

They ran to the golden door and Jayben frantically tried one of the keys in the lock. It wouldn't turn, so he tried another. And another . . .

The Agent on the ground moaned, slowly turning to face him.

'Hurry!' cried Peggro.

'Stand back,' said Phee, shoving Jayben to the side and raising her leg.

WHAM!

With one kick she busted the door open and they hurried through, into a corridor of marble sculptures. Phee shoved a heavy sculpture against the broken door just as the Agent hurled himself against it.

'Which way?' said Jayben, looking left and right.

They were hesitating, when Lulie Bean suddenly woke up, shot into the air and buzzed to the left, down the corridor. *Has she smelled candy again?* Jayben wondered, as she disappeared through an open door.

'Careful,' said Peggro, re-covering his face with the dragon silk to make himself completely invisible again. 'There will be lots more Agents, surely.'

Maybie followed Lulie Bean, turning left and flying down the corridor.

The others tiptoed behind her.

'Peggro?' Jayben whispered. 'Can you go ahead and check it out? They won't see you.'

'But I'll see them,' Peggro said, his voice trembling. 'I'm still scared.'

Jayben reached out to where Peggro had spoken from to reassure him, only to grasp air.

Then they heard Peggro whisper from down the corridor, 'Coast's clear.'

Jayben grinned, proud of his little brother, and they hurried through to find an enormous round hall with a grand staircase, flanked by two golden statues of Zamar, glistening in the sunshine from upstairs.

Phee wrinkled her nose at the statues' flexed arms and legs. 'Gross.'

'Mee-mow,' they heard Lulie Bean say from a sideboard in the corner. She was helping herself to a big bowl of sweets.

Maybie fluttered over to her. 'Well done for finding the stairs!'

It was eerily quiet. Where was everyone? Jayben didn't want to find out. 'It looked like Zamar's lift could go right to the top,' he said. 'So that's where we're going.'

They climbed to the first floor of the glass tower

to find another glass column of marbles at the centre of the building. A spiral staircase wound around it, all the way up.

'Up *there*?' asked Peggro, his face turning pale. 'It's too high!'

'It's the only way without being seen,' said Jayben, holding the purple monocle to his eye to look at the blinding sky through the glass surrounding them. The sun was even higher. The moon was no longer visible but he knew it was there, edging closer and closer into the sun's path. They had to hurry.

'Come on!' he said.

They started to climb, up and up, round and round. It was dizzying and exhausting and hot.

They stopped for a moment to catch their breath, trying not to look down.

Peggro removed the gown to cool off. 'What kind of person builds something like this?'

'A baddie,' said Maybie, buzzing to his side. 'Poor Peggro. You're doing so well. Nearly there.'

Jayben was trying not to look at the millions of marbles twinkling at them from inside the pillar. In his mind were the desperate faces of the people outside the gates, begging for a single marble, just so they could eat. His legs felt like jelly as they climbed higher and higher, until at last they reached the top floor.

Phee crawled on to a landing and into another corridor of golden doors. 'I never want to see stairs again in my entire life.'

They crept to the first door. Peggro draped himself with the cloak again and opened it a crack, to find a luxurious apartment with a stunning view of the glittering blue sea. There was nobody there, but Jayben spotted a marble table with gold legs. There was a map on it.

He walked over to have a look. The map was of the city and surrounding desert, where it showed several tombs dotted about in the sand. Someone had drawn a circle around one of them. It was twinkling yellow from inside.

Peggro pulled the cloak off his head. 'That's the one Null's headed to,' he said. 'Full of star glass.'

Jayben folded the map, stashing it in his pocket with his compass.

Suddenly Russog stirred. 'Oinff!' he said, a warning in his bark.

They turned and froze. Standing in the doorway was a group of bare-chested men, flashpins drawn. They had entered so quietly none of them had heard.

They were trapped.

In Maybie's voice, Russog screamed, 'I wanna fly home!'

The man in the middle smirked. 'Nice try, Imposter. This way . . .'

They had no choice but to obey, slowly shuffling past the armed men into the corridor.

Jayben whispered to the others, 'Don't worry – it'll be okay.' But, really, he wasn't sure how. The eclipse would happen any moment and they were powerless to stop Null from entering the tomb.

This is all my fault, Jayben thought miserably. He had insisted on coming to Zamar's palace to take the Torch back instead of going straight to the tomb. If they failed to stop Null, there was only himself to blame.

The golden doors were open now and as they were marched past one, they heard a familiar voice call out,

'Stop! Bring them to me.'

They were led into another lavish apartment, filled with statues of Zamar and draped with garish carpets. And there was Zamar himself, standing by an open balcony. He was waiting for his lift, which was being winched slowly up the chain towards him – and in his hand he clasped the Golden Torch.

CHAPTER 25

A Remarkable Gift

'Good to see you again, Dreamer,' said Zamar with a smirk. 'I was worried that we'd lost you after our skirmish in the cactus woods. That was upsetting.'

Jayben stood up straight. 'What would you care?' he said, looking the man in the eye. 'You wanted me dead.'

Zamar laughed over the rattling of the chains. 'Dead?' he said. 'I wanted to do a deal with you! You're the most powerful Dreamer in the world, aren't you?'

'You think I'm an imposter,' said Jayben suspiciously.

'I was never quite sure, although I went along with the other Dreamer, of course. But I admit, I was

curious about you. It's why I tracked you down in the Fairywood. When I saw what you were capable of . . . Well, it convinced me that perhaps you *are* the Ninth Dreamer. Now, we don't have long. I'd like to offer you a deal. An exchange.'

A deal? Jayben thought incredulously. *With Null's ally?* Never.

'I could never trust *you*. Not after the things you've done. Those poor kids you stole. You took their wings! You forced families from their homes! There are people out there starving because of you!'

Zamar shook his head. 'That was business, I'm afraid. I'm a reasonable guy. All that those Fairywood folk needed to do was accept me as their leader. They wouldn't see sense. But you're not stupid, are you, Dreamer? Sometimes, to get what you want, you have to give something up. Life's not a fairy tale.' He stroked the Golden Torch, gleaming in the sunshine. His eyes met Jayben's.

Was he offering to trade something for the Torch?

'Oinff!' said Russog, then in Mandon's voice he said, 'More like quarter to lunch, where you're sitting!'

More like quarter to lunch, where you're sitting. Jayben remembered Mandon saying those very words the previous day, not long before noon.

Russog was telling him the time. And time was running out.

'What sort of a deal are you suggesting?' Jayben asked, trying to buy some time to think.

'What are you doing?' Peggro whispered. 'You can't trust him.'

Zamar grinned, then pointed to a table on the balcony. There was a large red box with a lid on it. 'Take a look.'

He nodded to his men, and one of them lowered his weapon and shoved Jayben from behind in the direction of the box.

'Ben!' said Phee. 'It's not safe!'

'What choice do I have?' he said. He walked towards the table. Then he paused with his hand above the box. 'What is it?'

'Open it,' said Zamar.

Jayben could hear a man shouting from below the balcony.

'Heave!' the man yelled. 'Put your backs into it!'

Jayben peered over the ledge, looking down to the foot of the tower. In the courtyard he could see a circle of white dots – the lost children in their white gowns – arranged around a huge wheel.

'Harder!' the man shouted beside them.

They were turning the wheel, which Jayben could

now see was attached to the chains that were slowly pulling Zamar's heavy gold lift. And it was very nearly at the top.

Jayben was horrified and briefly distracted from the box. 'Those poor kids,' he said. 'How can you make them pull that thing?'

'Could we focus on what matters?' said Zamar. 'The box. In case you hadn't noticed, the eclipse is nearly upon us.'

Jayben took the purple lens from his pocket and looked up at the sun. There was already a nick in its surface, as if someone had taken a tiny bite out of it. The eclipse was happening!

Jayben grabbed the lid of the red box, throwing it open, and was nearly blinded by dazzling light from inside, sparkling in every colour. 'What the moon?' he said, looking away.

Zamar laughed. 'The biggest diamonds in Fellooz.'

'I don't understand.'

'Look at them,' Zamar said. 'And keep looking.'

Jayben squinted at the box of diamonds. There were dozens of them, and they were enormous – some as big as a gribblenut!

'Good,' said Zamar. 'Now. Don't look away. You have a gift, remember? A *remarkable* gift?'

A remarkable gift. Jayben felt goosebumps. He knew those words. He felt them. He remembered hearing them in that same voice, somewhere else . . .

And then a name came to him.

Marcus.

There was no face to the name, but the name was clear.

Who was Marcus? He stared at the diamonds.

He heard Zamar say, 'Remember the stocking, Ben?'

An image flashed up in Jayben's mind: a bright-red stocking, embroidered with a golden 'B' for Ben.

Ben.

Suddenly he knew that was his name in the Earth World – his earthling.

Ben.

The diamonds shook.

CRACK!

In a bright flash of light the box of diamonds turned into the stocking. Jayben gasped. He felt drawn to it and picked it up. It brought him an intense feeling of comfort and love and home.

'What is it, Jay-Jay?' said Maybie.

Zamar grinned. 'A fair trade. You'll have made my earthling very happy.' The winch made a screeching noise and the chain stopped. The lift had arrived. 'It's

a shame that you had to run off before. As I said, I was impressed by your powers in the woods. We could have stopped things at the tomb before the eclipse. Then, with your power, we could have been a team. But now it's too late.'

'What are you talking about?' said Jayben.

Zamar shook his head with a look of pity that was strangely familiar. He pointed to the window, to the sun. 'The eclipse has begun. The tables are about to turn back, and I can't afford to betray the one who'll be the most powerful Dreamer once again – who paid good money to have those crooked Guards get this Torch to me.' He put it on his belt.

'So it was a Guard!' Jayben felt sick. 'Who? Who was it? Tell me!'

Zamar just grinned and stepped inside the golden lift.

'You can't take the Torch to Null!'

'Like I said, it's just business.'

Zamar's shadow on the floor appeared slightly fainter now. The sky was already dimming.

Jayben heard the man from the courtyard calling out orders to the children: 'Hold it . . . Hold it . . .'

'No!' said Jayben. 'You know what Null will do with it. How can you call that *business*? It's people's lives! He'll wipe everyone's minds! Both worlds in darkness.'

Through his fear and rage Jayben noticed the air was twinkling and he looked at Maybie. She had edged closer to the ledge and was shaking her golden nutshell charm, emptying fairy dust over the side of the balcony, sending it drifting down to the kids in the courtyard.

'Life's not a fairy tale,' said Zamar, ringing a bell on the side of the golden lift. 'See you on the other side.'

And, just like that, it all fell into place.

Jayben knew that voice and that name. Marcus. Ben's cruel aunt's boyfriend – and Zamar's earthling.

The stocking. It was precious to Ben in the Earth World. Now it was here. But how? Jayben had unwittingly taken it from his earthling, swapping it for a box of diamonds. He thought back to the last words Zamar had said to him before the swap. *A remarkable gift.*

Somehow, those words had triggered the exchange. Zamar had sent his earthling self diamonds to make him rich in Earth World. But how had Zamar realised that would happen? How was Zamar able to remember his Earth self?

The questions swirled in his head. But one thing was certain. Zamar had the Golden Torch. With the power of the eclipse, Null could control the minds of two worlds.

He imagined his earthling self, bereft without his stocking. The feelings of frustration and loss from deep down were stronger than ever. Jayben now knew they were Ben's feelings. Anger shot through his brain and Jayben felt a surge of power.

His Trollwood charm lit up.

CHAPTER 26

The Tomb

'Look!' Maybie said, pointing down below.

White-gowned figures were drifting up in the glittering air, miniature children carried by silver wings. Maybie's dust had healed the Fairywood children, regrowing their wings and shrinking them down.

The man in the courtyard struggled to hold the wheel steady, staring in disbelief. He yelled, 'Stop! Where are you going? Take the wheel! *TAKE THE WHEEL!*'

Zamar, who had just stepped into the lift, looked bewildered. 'What's going on?' he demanded, as the lift swung in the air.

Jayben looked at the Torch on Zamar's belt and, channelling all of the rage he felt at its loss, all of his earthling self's hurt and pain, with all his will he ripped it away.

Zamar gasped as the winch jerked and the chains were released. 'NO!' he yelled, but before he could get off the lift, it dropped, free-falling.

Jayben caught the Torch in his hand.

There was a loud *BOOM!* from the courtyard and the chains of the lift were still. A cloud of dust obscured their vision.

Jayben spun round. Zamar's men were raising their flashpins, although they looked nervous. With one glance, Jayben whipped the flashpins from their hands.

'Go, Jay-Jay!' Maybie cheered.

But Jayben couldn't enjoy the victory. The sky was darkening, as if it was suddenly dusk. The eclipse was happening. How were they going to get to the tomb in time? Null would be there by now, surely – and even without the Torch, Null's powers would be immense if he touched those gems at the right moment.

Raynor was right, Jayben thought desperately. He had been so focused on getting the Torch that he had endangered them all. He looked around the apartment as Zamar's men backed away. There was nothing that could help – just hideous furniture, statues and a few small carpets, the size of doormats . . .

Wait. *Doormats?* He remembered the tall slide they would ride down to school in Ampelwed. Without another thought, he grabbed a carpet and chucked Phee and Peggro one each.

'Let's go!'

He rushed past the men, handing the stocking to Phee as they ran.

'Can you put that in your backpack?' he gasped, as they hurried back to the top of the stairs. 'It's precious to someone.'

She nodded and thrust it into her backpack, buckling it up firmly.

'You've got to be kidding me!' cried Peggro, as Jayben threw his carpet down on the top step. 'As if going up wasn't bad enough!'

'Let's do it!' Jayben said, sitting down and grabbing the front of the carpet.

WHOOSH! He shot down the spiral staircase. '*Whoa!*' he yelled, thrilled and terrified all at once as he picked up speed, barely touching the steps, whipping round the turns. He could hear the others wailing behind him and Russog farting continuously over every bump.

'I'm gonna throw up!' Peggro cried as they reached the bottom, gliding across the shiny floor before slamming awkwardly into a statue.

Phee laughed. 'Russog, you are disgusting!'

'Charming!' Russog replied in Larnie's voice.

Through some tall glass doors Jayben could see a gold chariot, chained to a skallabore drinking from a trough. They sprinted through the doors and leapt on to it.

Jayben took the reins and gave the creature a tap, but it didn't move. He could see scars on its back from where it had been whipped. Maybie fluttered down to join them on the chariot.

He passed the map from Zamar's desk to Peggro and his compass to Phee. 'Hold on tight,' he said. With one hand on the reins, he held up the Golden Torch and said, '*Wish this.*'

BOOOOOM!

The flames exploded from the Torch and the skallabore launched into a gallop.

'AAAH!' Peggro screamed, clinging to his brother as they hurtled back towards the procession of glass columns filled with marbles. In his mind, Jayben saw those hungry faces and empty hands outstretched. He swung the Torch to the left as they passed the first column. The glass cracked with the heat of the flames. He swung to the right, catching the next one. The enormous glass pillars shattered, flooding the gardens with millions of marbles.

Phee gently punched Jayben's shoulder. 'Nice one, Ben!'

They were fast approaching the gates, and the Agents guarding them.

Jayben looked at their flashpins and sent them flying into the flower beds.

'Open the gates!' he yelled.

Looking terrified, they flung the gates open and dived out of their path.

The skallabore thundered out, followed by waves of marbles, spilling out of the glass city and into the streets, taking the Agents with them.

The Torch went out, hissing and smoking, but the skallabore kept running.

'South-west!' Peggro shouted, clutching the map, and Jayben tugged the left rein, turning the creature, and headed for the open desert.

The air felt cooler now and the sand wasn't quite so bright. Peggro held the lens to his eye, looking to the sun. 'It's half covered already!'

Jayben spotted something in the desert ahead: the

grey, square tomb. As they galloped closer, a line of vehicles came into view, parked outside. Nine four-wheeled cars with steam billowing from their funnels. Jayben had never seen anything like them in the Elf World before. They were empty, but a group of Agents were standing by the tomb's dark entrance.

Jayben felt sick. 'He's already in there!'

The light grew dimmer.

'What now?' cried Peggro.

'There's still time,' said Phee, her expression determined. 'It's not a total eclipse yet. The gems can't help Null until it's just that ring of light.'

'You can do it, Jay-Jay,' said Maybie, flying by his shoulder. 'You can still stop him.'

The skallabore began to slow, without the fear of the Torch's flame.

Jayben looked at the tomb with trepidation. Its ominous doorway appeared much bigger as they neared, like a monster's gaping mouth, ready to swallow him. But there was no taming the beast that was his fate. To save the light, the Energy of two worlds, he needed to face the darkness.

Gritting his teeth, he pushed the Torch down in his pocket and felt the star glass gem. However it got in his pocket, it felt like a sign. He was meant to do this. He fixed his eyes on the nearing Agents. 'Everyone ready?' he said.

'About as unready as I'll ever be,' said Peggro, vanishing under the dragon-silk gown.

The skallabore began to turn. They leapt from the chariot and the Agents drew their weapons . . .

Jayben looked at their flashpins and, one by one, he sent them flying. Only one Agent clung on to his now. Jayben stared at the barrel but it wouldn't move. Jayben's charm had dimmed again.

Then something else knocked it out of the Agent's hand.

'Ouch!' he heard Peggro moan. 'That was harder than I thought.'

'Go, Peggro!' Maybie cheered, as Phee tripped the Agent over.

The other Agents backed away and, with a deep breath, Jayben walked gingerly into the tomb.

There was a smell of damp and a chill in the air, colder with every step he took into the darkness. As his eyes adjusted, he could see that the huge stones in the walls, each one thicker than a tree trunk, were engraved with tiny drawings of krizzards, rawks and skallabores, painted in gold.

He felt Lulie Bean hiding in his pocket and Peggro

grabbing the back of his shirt as the darkness enveloped them.

Jayben looked down and could just about see the top of a wide stone staircase in the failing light from the entrance. Phee held his arm, Maybie landed on his shoulder and they warily took the first step down.

The air grew colder still. The scrapes of their sandals echoed against the stone, but they couldn't see a thing in the pitch black. Where were the star glass gems? Where was Null? They took another step down and the smell of damp was stronger.

Russog starting burping nervously and in Tedrik's voice he said, 'Stay here, boy.' It echoed back to them. '*Stay here, boy . . . Stay here, boy . . .*'

Phee and Peggro held out their charms but their gentle glow wasn't enough to reveal their surroundings. Jayben couldn't risk lighting the Torch in case it attracted Null's attention.

Then he had another idea. 'The bookle bug!' he said.

Peggro opened his satchel and, sure enough, the bug was shining from inside, clinging to a book.

Jayben lifted the book slowly, illuminating the stairs and some of the sandy stone floor below. He imagined the tomb as like any of the fierce beasts he had faced before. He would show it no fear. He stood up straight and continued down, pausing at the bottom in the eerie silence. The air here had a fierce chill to it. He could just see the shimmer of gold engravings of rawks on a stone wall. Then he saw a shadow move. He let out a breath as the silhouette of a person emerged.

Peggro gripped him tighter and Maybie buried her face against his neck.

Russog burped and Phee whispered with a quiver, 'Who is that?'

The figured shuffled nearer but there was no response. Jayben's heart thumped in his chest as he braced himself, preparing to see the white masked face of Null in that black hooded cloak.

But instead, a woman with red hair appeared, dressed in a white gown. Her face wore no expression but her lips were moving, uttering a few words in another language: Null's whispers.

Jayben knew that only adults could be affected by the whispers but that didn't make it any less scary to see. Other figures emerged – dozens more of them, all in white gowns, shuffling and whispering the curse with the same vacant expression.

'So this is the *special place* Zamar was sending nullheads? To the tomb?' He shook his head. 'They're people – sons, daughters, mums and dads. She might have been a marshal. He might have been a teacher. They had homes and friends. Null's robbed them of everything!'

Phee put her arm around his shoulder. 'I know, Ben. And keeping them down *here*? It's beyond cruel.'

Instead of fear, Jayben now felt rage. Null needed to be stopped, once and for all.

'Where is he?' he said, nostrils flaring. 'The eclipse is gonna happen any moment. We *can't* let him get to the gems.'

They walked on, carefully dodging the nullheads, until they heard a strange noise from a corridor, like the rustling of a thousand dry leaves blowing in the wind. The sound grew louder until—

'AAAH!' Peggro cried, as a cloud of large flying insects swarmed, buzzing, out of the passage.

Everyone raised their arms, ducking to avoid them, but there were too many.

One landed on Jayben's arm. It was the size of his foot, with the body of a locust and the head of a small lizard with red eyes, snapping its teeth with a screech. Around its body was a gold ring. Another crawled up his leg and one pounced on his shoulder. They were all wearing gold rings.

'Snippids!' Peggro cried. 'This can't be real! It's a nightmare!'

'Get off!' shouted Phee, as one bit into her arm and Russog squirmed in her backpack.

Jayben felt Maybie trying to squish into his pocket with Lulie Bean. He jumped around, trying to swat the creatures away. Just as the hum became deafening, the pests fell away and flew backwards up the corridor, as if sucked by a vacuum, disappearing into an open door. As the last one disappeared, he noticed a dark figure by the door, with a glowing blue charm. He felt a shiver down his spine.

Null?

CHAPTER 27

Total Eclipse

A huge stone door slid across, shutting the pests inside. The dark figure stepped forward, Trollwood charm glowing. Jayben stood firm, even though his heart was thudding. The figure took another step forward and another—

'Good grief,' said the figure. 'Those creatures were *most* unpleasant.'

Jayben gasped. He knew that voice.

The figure lit a lantern, and there was no white mask or black hood. Instead, Jayben saw a long white beard and rosy, wrinkled cheeks – an old man in a cream shirt and trousers, clutching a cane.

'*Grandpa?*' said Jayben. 'Grandpa Mandon! Are you okay?'

'Fine, thank you, dear boy,' his grandpa said, removing one earplug. 'It's *you* I've been worried about. I knew you would be racing to get here. I wish I'd been here sooner but a momple can only walk so fast. Are you hurt?'

'No – but how did you get rid of them? And how did you escape from Zamar's men? We were captured!' asked Jayben.

'Magic! It's a good job those revolting snippids are so fond of wearing gold!' He waved his glowing charm with a twinkle in his eye. 'Anything made of metal or rock, remember? Zamar's men weren't interested in an old man like me; they ran right past me.'

Phee said warningly, 'The eclipse is nearly complete. We don't have much time.'

Jayben pulled himself together, checking his star glass was safely in his pocket. 'Where are all the other gems?' he asked his grandpa.

'This way,' said Mandon, putting his earplugs back in. He raised his lantern and led the way further into the tomb.

Seeing his grandpa's charm shining so brightly, it was hard not to feel frustrated by the dwindling light of his own charm. 'My magic's weak again,' Jayben said.

Mandon patted him on the back. 'Don't you worry. It'll still bring you luck.'

Jayben wasn't so sure about that. 'I felt some power when I got the Torch back from Zamar in the city, but now it's weak again. With those crystals stuck in the Earth World, I'll be no match for Null if he gets the star glass.'

Mandon shook his head. 'Until that happens, you are still the most powerful Dreamer. Let's keep it that way.'

'Oinff!' said Russog, then in Mandon's voice he said, *'There are things you're much better off not knowing.'*

'What's that, boy?' said Phee as they hurried on.

'This way, this way,' said Mandon.

'I know what Russog means,' said Maybie, peeping out of Jayben's pocket. 'He's repeating what you said yesterday, Mandon, when we were talking about the coded message in the suitcase. The first words in capital letters were DAUGHTER, JOURNEYS, DISGUISE? No, that can't be right. How did it start?'

Right on cue, Russog opened his snout and recited in Jayben's voice, emphasising the words in capital letters:

A message from the chief's DAUGHTER:

Two of our guards IN the jungle, hunting for the witch in DISGUISE, had their JOURNEYS disrupted by a sea monster. They retreated TO avoid watery GRAVES. Now a fresh sighting OF the witch is reported at the GOLDEN cliffs - details in the GLASS bottle. The guards will resume their mission WHEN the MOON is full. They will meet the wizard where the sea BLOCKS the caves the next DAY. To STOP the witch HER powers must be disabled. For the right price the wizard AT the caves will rid her of ALL magic. They will advise the COST in due course.

'Wow, Russog!' said Jayben. 'That was a lot!'

'So, wait,' said Peggro. 'The words are DAUGHTER IN DISGUISE JOURNEYS . . .'

'Yes!' said Phee. 'Then it's TO GRAVES OF GOLDEN GLASS.'

'Graves of golden glass?' said Jayben. 'Like the tomb? Of star glass?'

'WHEN MOON BLOCKS DAY,' added Maybie.

'The eclipse!' Jayben put the final words together. 'STOP HER AT ALL COST.' Jayben felt a rush of goosebumps. 'Stop who? Whose daughter?'

Mandon didn't seem to hear them, marching

forward with his earplugs in, approaching the bottom of some stone steps.

An uneasy feeling settled in Jayben's stomach. What wasn't Mandon telling him, and why?

'Now, let me do the talking up here,' said Mandon. 'Stay behind me.'

Climbing the steps, Jayben looked up and gasped. It was dark but there was no roof, only the night sky – at midday. He took out the purple lens. The final glimmer of the sun had just disappeared behind the moon. The others raced up the steps, speechless.

Mandon whispered, 'Here it comes . . .'

Three breaths later, the moon became a shimmering halo of light.

Total eclipse.

'Whoa!' said Jayben, as the tomb's pillars were tinted pink.

Something sparkled on the other side of the courtyard, a yellow gem. It was a star glass, in gloved hands.

Jayben's stomach dropped as someone in a black hooded cloak emerged from the shadows. A white mask of porcelain stared, depicting a face with no expression, and large black eye holes with no visible eyes behind them.

Null.

'We meet again, Imposter,' Null said in the strange, distorted voice of the mask.

Null's Trollwood charm shone brightly and suddenly the Torch in Jayben's pocket was yanked with such force that he was dragged to the ground before it was torn from his shorts, flying through the air and into Null's gloved hand.

'NO!' cried Jayben, scrambling to his feet. Just like that, the Torch was gone. Null was more powerful than Jayben had expected.

Null howled with laughter and before Jayben could take out his star glass, a slab of stone was turned into a huge brass station clock, then thrown at him – hard – pinning him against a pillar and crushing his leg. Jayben's star glass gem fell from his torn pockets and bounced a few feet away, before shimmering in the light of the eclipse.

'STOP!' Peggro shouted, coughing in a cloud of dust.

'BEN!' Phee screamed from the steps.

'We're coming for you, Jay-Jay!' cried Maybie.

Mandon walked towards Jayben. 'Leave the boy alone,' he said. 'This has to stop.'

A tall, broken pillar of stone was knocked down, crashing between them and Jayben.

Jayben heaved with all his might to move the clock

but it was just too heavy. All he could do was watch the star glass in Null's glove, shining brighter and brighter in the light of the eclipse.

'Drop it!' he cried. 'You don't deserve this power!'

Null lifted a sleeve to reveal the remaining dark Rainbow crystals. 'You tried to steal my powers, Dreamer,' Null whispered. 'Now watch me become more powerful than you could ever imagine.'

Jayben could only look on helplessly as Null pressed the star glass against the Rainbow crystals and, with a loud hiss, the yellow gem shone.

Null raised the Torch.

'*Wish this . . .*'

THUD! THUD! THUD! THUD!

Darkning struck all around.

Pillars cracked. Shards of ice rained down.

'Time to finish what I started!' Null howled. 'Time to take control of not just one world, but two!'

The Golden Torch gave off blue sparks as it sucked the light from the sky.

Null had begun to close the pipeline.

Everything seemed to happen in slow motion. Jayben craned his neck to see his friends, brother and grandpa collapsing to the ground. The Energy was draining away.

'STOP!' he shouted, desperately writhing to free himself, but the enormous clock was crushing him. Its ticking pierced his head.

Tick tick tick.

His arm began to tingle. His head ached.

THUD! THUD! THUD!

The darkning continued and black clouds appeared, swirling above and blocking the ring of light. Null held up the Torch and laughed.

Jayben stretched his arm out for the star glass, but it was out of reach. He heaved with all his might but the clock wouldn't budge. He let out a cry and tears filled his eyes. He was trapped. Powerless to stop Null while he wiped the memories of everyone in both worlds.

All that love and friendship . . . lost.

And Jayben was responsible. He had insisted on going after the Torch. If only they had come straight to the tomb. If only he hadn't trusted that witch back in the market. If only he hadn't Free-Dreamed those crystals away. In his mind he could still see the wand full of crystals, taunting him.

Tick tick tick

And then it dawned on him.

Those crystals.

He had sent those crystals to Earth. Weak and scared though he had been, he had done it. *What if . . .* he wondered.

He delved into his pocket, pulling out the pencil. A plain grey pencil. The plainest Earthly object you could imagine. Then he pictured Terrisell's wand. For a moment he couldn't remember it, and then he imagined himself back into her cluttered little grotto, remembered the moment the crystals had been stripped from him. It swam into focus – a glowing stick, encrusted with dark Rainbow crystals. He could see it, as clear as day. Every twisted line in the wood. Every fault in the crystals.

The pencil shook and—

CRACK!

In a bright flash of light the ordinary pencil turned into the wand, the Rainbow crystals embedded, exactly as it had been.

Jayben had swapped it back.

He'd spent so long believing he needed to wait for something to bring out his powers, to control them, believing that without the Torch he was nothing. But he'd had the power all along. The power to change his fate.

He was no longer trapped. No longer helpless.

The clock stopped ticking.

From behind it, he heard Null laughing at the black sky. 'The pipeline is nearly sealed! Looks like you're out of luck, Imposter!'

Jayben recalled Captain Winnibar's hoarse voice quoting the Seventh Dreamer: *You won't need luck if you refuse to lose.*

The words spoke to him again. Jayben hadn't come here to give up. He felt a surge of power from deep inside and the dark Rainbow crystals in the wand detached, as if pulled magnetically by the Rainbow crystals in his palm.

I refuse to lose, he thought.

The dark crystals rushed through the air, each one returning to his hand. His Trollwood charm lit up once more, glowing strong, a bright-blue light in the darkness.

His old magic was coursing through his veins, the magic of his Trollwood ancestors. Of the family he couldn't remember but knew he had.

Jayben looked at the clock's big face and, with the force of his mind, sent it flying off him, through the air, and—

SLAM!

It hit Null, knocking the Torch to the floor.

With a groan of determination, Jayben pushed off from the pillar and limped towards his gleaming star glass. He picked it up, and as his Rainbow crystals made contact, the yellow gem hissed and shone.

'Aaah!' he yelled as the power shot through him. It was overwhelming, like electricity. He suddenly felt like he was ten feet taller and he straightened up. The crystals in his hand flickered wildly as he turned to face Null, who was slowly sitting up. The Torch leapt off the ground and flew into Jayben's hand.

'*Wish this*,' he said.

The darkning ceased, then sparks flew from the Torch.

Behind the mask, Null watched. There was a crack down the middle of the porcelain face.

BOOOOOM!

Flames erupted in the air, shaking the pillars and illuminating every corridor of the tomb. The swirling clouds above them rippled with purple lightning, before the Torch suddenly puffed out.

'Ben?' he heard Phee say. His friends were coming to, staggering to their feet.

He kept his eye firmly on Null.

From behind the cracked mask somebody spoke –

but they sounded very different now, like the device had been broken.

'You'll regret that,' said Null. Their voice was higher.

Jayben frowned. 'Who are you?'

Null raised an arm and sent a rock flying towards Jayben, but before it could hit him, Jayben looked at it and it shattered in mid-air. Null raised a hand and another rock lifted into the air—

'Leave him alone, Ellissam!'

Jayben turned to see Mandon, Phee and Peggro pulling themselves up.

'Ellissam?' asked Jayben, puzzled.

Mandon put his arm around Jayben, facing Null. His voice was gentle but firm as he said, 'This madness has to stop. Everything you're doing, in the name of your absurd ambitions, must stop. You have destroyed too many lives.'

'Not a chance,' said Null.

'Grandpa?' Jayben said, looking between them, confused. 'Do you know Null? Who is Ellissam?'

Null laughed. Their voice – a woman's voice, Jayben thought – rang out high and clear. 'You must be so proud, Mandon, to have found the Dreamer the Book always wanted.'

There was something *familiar* about her voice.

'And a boy,' she continued. 'Just like the Book said. Shame he isn't family.'

Mandon grinned. 'Oh, but he is.' He looked proudly at his grandson in the flashes of purple lightning. 'And he has his mother's eyes.'

Jayben could only watch, bewildered, as the figure slowly removed the damaged mask, which must have distorted her voice, to reveal long black hair, a thin angular face and piercing green eyes. She looked startled. 'Family?' she cried. 'No. He can't be.'

'That's right,' said Mandon. 'The Dreamer is family to us both.'

Null had recovered herself. 'You lie,' she said with a scowl.

'I'm not lying, Ellissam,' Mandon said, his voice still gentle.

He heard Russog. 'Oinff! Oinff!' And again, in Mandon's voice he said, *'There are things you're much better off not knowing.'*

Then suddenly the penny dropped. The decoded message:

DAUGHTER IN DISGUISE
JOURNEYS TO GRAVES OF GOLDEN GLASS
WHEN MOON BLOCKS DAY

STOP HER AT ALL COST

The message was for Mandon.

Mandon's daughter in disguise.

Null was in disguise. Ellissam was Null.

There was a crash of thunder and Jayben went cold as it hit him like a rock.

Null was his aunt.

CHAPTER 28

One Last Nullhead

'You can't be my aunt!' Jayben said, feeling physically sick. To be related to Null, the cruel destroyer of so many lives, who had taken Phee's father and his own – no, he wouldn't believe it. He turned to Mandon. 'You knew, all along? Why didn't you tell me?'

Mandon looked pained. 'I wanted to. Had we not been separated back in Karassan—'

Another crash of thunder and a hot wind blew.

Null shook her head. 'Related to that wretched child? Never.'

'It's true,' said Mandon. 'In both worlds. Whether you like it or not, we are family.'

Maybie fluttered next to Jayben. 'She can't be Null. Null's a man, isn't he?'

Peggro stood up, scratching his head. 'The Book said the Ninth Dreamer would be a boy. And Null wanted people to believe they were the Ninth . . .'

'That's why you wore the mask?' said Phee, her nostrils flaring. 'So you could con your supporters into believing you're the *Ninth*? To get them to help you – help you hurt so many people?' Her red charm glowed as she shook with anger. She lifted a slab of stone . . .

Null simply flicked her wrist and the stone flew backwards into a pillar, dragging Phee with it.

'Phee!' cried Jayben.

Null laughed. 'Hopeless.'

Hopeless.

A name shot into Jayben's head. A name from another world.

Samantha.

An image flashed into his mind along with it – *angular face, green eyes watching him coldly.* It brought the most ferocious wave of fury.

His Rainbow crystals flickered erratically and every stone in the tomb began to shake as images flashed into his mind.

A kitchen; sweeping up. A stack of homework. A walk to school. A dark classroom – and he was locked in—

CRACK!

One of the pillars turned into a dishwasher.

CRACK!

Another became a lamp post, bowing under the weight of the roof.

CRACK! CRACK! CRACK!

A bus stop, a fridge, a school desk.

The thunder crashed and the tomb began to crumble.

'Jayben!' cried Phee. 'Stop!'

Jayben struggled to stop the Free-Dreams appearing, but his anger was uncontrolled; a terrifying, wild power. His grandpa took his arm.

'Hurry, my boy,' he cried. 'We must run, while we can.'

But Jayben couldn't stop. Free-Dreams collided with pillars, sending dust and stone flying. Null's eyes darted around the disintegrating pillars, rocks tumbling – then she turned and ran.

CRACK!

The pillar in front of her turned into a huge dustcart, spilling bags of rubbish everywhere.

She turned, scanning desperately for a way out. Jayben took another step towards her, and another. This woman might be his aunt, but he had no feeling for her except hatred. She had destroyed so many lives and now she would pay . . .

'Let's get her!' said Maybie, buzzing forward.

With one quick glance, Null swept the piece of star glass on the ground into the air – sending it hurtling right at Maybie. Before Jayben could stop it, the glass had struck Maybie, knocking her out of the air.

The fairy let out a faint cry and crumpled to the ground.

With a short laugh, Null whipped away, down the steps.

'*Maybie!*' Jayben yelled, forgetting about Null, rushing to scoop his tiny friend into his hands. She felt cold and lifeless. 'Wake up, Maybie!' he cried, as the others gathered around. 'Please, Maybie! Wake up!'

The wind whipped sand into his face and the dark sky rumbled above. Tears filled his eyes. Null had claimed another victim. Maybie was gone.

And then, something amazing happened.

Glowing specks appeared and drifted through the air like dust, settling on Maybie's head.

Everyone was speechless.

Maybie suddenly gasped for a breath and sat up. 'Jay-Jay?'

Jayben beamed, holding her close. 'You're all right, Maybie!' he cried. 'But what happened? Gold specks are *your* magic, aren't they? How did *I* summon it?'

'Your charm,' said Maybie.

Jayben looked and was shocked to see that his blue charm was now glowing gold too. He had somehow gained the old magic of Fairywoods too.

There was a loud bang and one side of the tomb started to cave in.

'We need to go – now!' Mandon shouted. Jayben grabbed his star glass in one hand, the Torch in the other. They limped across the shaking courtyard.

'The whole place is crumbling!' cried Peggro.

'The pillars are falling here too,' said Phee. 'The entire courtyard will be rubble.'

'This way!' said Mandon, holding his lamp and cane and ducking to avoid falling rock. They ran down the steps where Null had also vanished.

There was no sign of her, but they had only run a few paces when they heard a familiar, dreadful sound. The buzz of snippids, escaping through cracks to swipe at their faces, snapping and screeching.

'We're nearly there,' gasped Mandon, urging everyone to the end of the corridor where they could see faint daylight.

But Phee had skidded to a halt. 'Wait – the nullheads!' she cried. 'They're still inside. They'll be crushed! We need to—'

She broke off as they saw people in white gowns fleeing up the steps, into the returning light. They were crying out, their voices afraid but clear and strong.

'They're free!' cried Maybie. 'But how?'

'The Torch,' gasped Phee, as she scrambled over rubble. 'The Torch's light and the Energy from it must have flooded the tomb. It set them free, just like at Last Rock last year when you freed those nullheads there, Ben. But Energy from the Free-Dream set your family free too, Maybie. All that Energy must be linked!'

'Hurry!' said Peggro, rushing to the steps. The rubble was falling faster now – they didn't have long.

Jayben's friends dashed towards freedom – but halfway up the steps he noticed one last nullhead, still standing in the shadows, facing away.

'Hey!' he shouted, his arm shielding his eyes from the sand that was pouring from the cracking roof. 'You need to leave! Now!'

The figure didn't move. They must have escaped the burst of light and Energy from the Torch.

Jayben looked up to the daylight, then back down at the nullhead, consigned to the darkness by Null's curse. He couldn't abandon them. They deserved a chance at life as much as anyone.

'I'm coming! Hang on!' And he turned from the daylight, hurrying down, back into the tomb.

'BEN!' Phee screamed from the top of the steps, as the others fled the crumbling building. 'What are you doing?'

Jayben hobbled towards the nullhead, dodging the falling debris. The figure was tall, with broad shoulders. Reaching them, Jayben gasped to see a man with chocolate-brown eyes, freckled cheeks and a greying brown beard. It couldn't be – and yet –

'Tedrik?' he whispered with tears in his eyes. He was thin but there was no mistaking his kind, worn face. The star glass fell from Jayben's hand as he took Tedrik's. 'Tedrik, it's me! Jayben!'

There was no response. Tedrik's arm was limp. He stared ahead with no expression, whispering the curse.

'Tedrik, please!' Jayben gently shook him. 'We need to go!'

Still nothing.

There was a terrible groan and Jayben looked round in time to see a section of wall falling towards them. He flung out a hand, when Phee suddenly appeared, catching the wall and holding it back with all her strength.

'Dad?' she said, gazing at Tedrik like she'd seen a ghost.

'Oinff!' said Russog from her backpack.

What can we do? Jayben thought frantically. If the burst of Energy from the Torch hadn't reached Tedrik, then what?

Russog spoke in Tedrik's deep voice, 'Always check your pockets . . .'

It was the start of the Feller family motto, Jayben remembered.

'Always check your pockets,' he whispered. 'Remember, Tedrik? Always check your pockets . . .'

Phee joined in. 'Always check your pockets . . .'

Phee began to weep, struggling to hold the stone back.

'Always check your pockets . . .'

Then Jayben noticed Tedrik's hand slowly slipping into the pocket of his white gown.

He had stopped whispering.

Then he blinked and said, 'Always check your

pockets . . . before you search the woods.' He glanced down at Jayben, eyebrows raised. 'Well, well. Jayben.'

'TEDRIK!' Jayben beamed, landing a giant hug on him. 'We have to go!' He grabbed his friend's arm and tugged him towards the steps, shoving him forward.

Phee let go of the wall, hurrying to support her dad as they raced towards the entrance.

Limping with his wounded leg, Jayben fell behind. He tripped under the doorframe, just as the entire building imploded into a cloud of dust.

'AAAH!' he yelled as rubble fell on him.

He felt eager hands cleaning away the rocks, dragging him free.

There were drops of violet rain falling on his dusty head. The wind dropped, the purple lightning ceased and the cloud emptied, drenching everyone.

'You're all right, dear boy,' said Mandon, smoothing Jayben's hair from his face.

'Let's get him to the city, quickly,' said Phee.

Jayben knew his leg was injured, it must be, but he couldn't feel the pain, he only knew that he was limping. Giddy with shock, he broke into laughter, overcome with relief and elation to see Tedrik and so many other nullheads freed at last, dancing in the rain as the sunshine re-emerged from the eclipse.

He raised his head. His vision blurred, but in the distance he could see the steaming funnels of the cars speeding away – Null and her Agents, fleeing into the desert.

As Tedrik, Mandon and Phee lifted him on to the back of Mandon's momple, he worried about what Null's next move could be, now that she had regained some power.

But it could wait. Seeing the Torch safely back in his hand, his charm glowing and his crystals shining bright, he just smiled. He saw a rainbow appearing over Zamar's city – and everything went dark.

'Morning, lad,' said a deep voice.

Jayben opened his eyes and was delighted to see Tedrik, looking more himself, the colour back in his cheeks in the light of a stove, where he was devouring a hot cropple cone. Jayben sat up with a grin, to find himself on a bed of pillows in Captain Winnibar's library on the rocking deck of the *Beth Rose*.

'Didn't I tell you?' he heard the captain squawk. 'You didn't need luck at all! You won't need luck . . .'

'If you refuse to lose,' he whispered. He saw the twinkle of her eye across the room, among the glowing shelves of bookles. The beams of the ship were peaceful now and from below deck he could hear the singing shells belting out a jolly tune.

Phee came hurrying through a doorway, followed by Peggro, Maybie, Russog, Mandon and Raynor.

'Ben!' said Phee, kneeling beside him and holding out a sweet cropple cone. 'You okay? We put you on the floor as you kept falling out of your hammock.'

He grinned and took the cone, realising he was fully healed. 'Much better. Thanks.'

'My dear boy,' said Mandon, his long white beard now tucked into a woolly cream cardigan. 'It's good to see you awake. I owe you an apology for keeping secrets. I would like to tell you everything, if you'll let me. You must have so many questions.'

But Jayben was busy checking his pockets. The Torch was there. 'Phew!' he sighed.

'Check the other one!' said Peggro.

Jayben pulled out a shiny new crystal shilling.

'Sourced it yesterday,' said Raynor. 'Right before the eclipse. Now you can hide your light from the Agents again, and no more random nightmares – *if* you can resist going for impromptu swims in the frozen sea . . .'

Jayben grinned. 'Thanks, Raynor. I think I'm learning to control my powers a bit.'

'Tell that to the tomb at Fellooz,' muttered Peggro, and they all laughed.

'Lulie Bean is staying home for a while,' said Maybie, giving Jayben a hug. 'She's taking the longest nap ever!'

'Oinff! Oinff!' said Russog, bounding on to Jayben's lap to lick his chin with his wet snout. Then he sang in Larnie's voice, *'Breakfaaast!'*

Jayben beamed, giving him an affectionate belly scratch. It brought back happy memories of the Fellers' quirky home in the Giantwood forest: a place of warmth and stability. But nothing was going to be the same now, not since learning about Zamar and his aunt.

'You're right,' he said, turning to his Grandpa Mandon. 'I do have questions. Lots of them.'

Mandon looked down. 'Fire away, dear boy.'

'Is Null . . . really my aunt?'

Mandon nodded. He looked sad and tired. 'She is, Jayben. Her name is Ellissam. I didn't know how to tell you something like that. Your mother's sister, capable of such things . . . But it's true. She and your mother Merriju were always very different, but in adulthood they took totally separate paths and held such starkly different beliefs. It's a long story but Ellissam became fanatical and we became estranged.

'Null, as she is now known to most, has always been obsessed with the prophesy of the Ninth Dreamer of *The Book of Dreamers*. But, of course, the Ninth Dreamer was predicted to be a boy, a child – Null is an adult. She decided to pretend. She got involved with that awful witch Snaggis seven years ago, who taught her how to use dark northern magic to bend others to her will. All it took was a mask and . . . the rest you know. It's a trick, plain and simple, a terrible disguise to achieve such power. I've used my position in the Guard to try and help those my daughter has hurt. And my fellow Guards thought I might be able to reason with her. That's why they sent me the message in the desert that you saw, just as they sent you to try to prevent her from entering. She really is hell-bent on breaking the Torch to gain total control over both worlds. Madness.'

'She won't get it again,' said Phee grimly.

Jayben nodded. 'I'm going to break the giant's spell. I'm sure the missing pages from *The Book of Dreamers* have the skeleton key words on them. I'm going to find those missing pages and light the Torch for good. That way, everyone's memories and magic will be restored for ever.'

He noticed something red sticking out of Peggro's satchel. It was the stocking marked with a golden 'B', and he remembered the diamonds he'd sent to the Earth World, tricked by Zamar.

'I knew their voices,' he said slowly, pulling out the stocking. 'Zamar and Null. I *know* them.' The names *Marcus* and *Samantha* drifted into his mind. 'From the other side.'

Raynor nodded. 'I'm afraid she is your aunt on both sides,' she said. 'Our earthling families are reflections of our families here. Sometimes even friendships, according to the ancient scholars.'

Jayben swallowed. 'I think Null's earthling is called Samantha,' he said. 'She – she's my legal guardian.' He fought down panic. 'What about *my* earthling? What if those people – Marcus and Samantha – know that he's *me*, and they harm him in the other world?'

Mandon shook his head, lost in thought. 'It can't be. People can't recognise faces between worlds, even if they remember other details.'

'But Zamar knew about an object that my earthling would know – the stocking. He knew it was precious to me, in Earth World. He said it was a *deal* and then he tricked me. He triggered me somehow into Free-Dreaming the diamonds to the Earth World. Afterwards he said, "You'll have made my earthling very happy."'

'So he must know your earthling,' said Peggro, looking scared. 'If he took the stocking from them in Earth World.'

'But how can Zamar connect to his earthling like that?' said Jayben, bewildered. 'If he's not a Dreamer? If he doesn't have Rainbow crystals then he's not a Dreamer, right?'

Mandon looked up. 'There *is* another way. It's recorded in *The Book of Dreamers*. Several centuries ago, an earthling was scratched by a snippid that had been Free-Dreamed to the Earth World. It's said that he could remember both his elfling and earthling self, without being a true Dreamer. Perhaps Zamar's earthling had an encounter with a Free-Dreamed creature.'

Jayben remembered something. 'The hemnik,' he said. 'I accidentally swapped a hemnik with a car when I first faced Null. Wait. It was *Marcus's* car! Marcus is Zamar's earthling! It bit Marcus . . .'

'Oh dear,' Mandon said. 'I suppose that's how it happened. This Marcus suddenly knew about Elf World and his elfling self and . . .'

Jayben felt slightly sick. 'So my earthling's in danger. If Marcus knows he's a Dreamer, then surely—'

'Now, now,' said his grandpa. 'Don't you worry. Your earthling will have the same powers as you – he'll be fine. And in the Earth World, who is this Marcus? Is he powerful?'

'N-no,' said Jayben uncertainly. 'Not really. He's Samantha's boyfriend.'

'Let's not forget, you brought that wand back from Earth, and put those Rainbow crystals back in your hand. You have twice as many crystals as Null, and with the boost from the star glass you are now the most powerful Dreamer ever to have lived.' Mandon's eyes were shining. 'You took control. There's nothing you can't do.'

'That's right,' said Peggro stoutly, and Phee nodded.

'You brought me back to life,' added Maybie.

'I know I can Free-Dream,' said Jayben. 'But I don't remember everything and until I do, I won't have my full powers.' He turned to Raynor, frustrated. 'Why haven't all my memories come back? Why can't I remember my parents?'

'The full moon,' said Raynor. 'You still haven't seen it in this world, have you – you only glimpsed it last year. It was enough for you to unlock your powers, but you're yet to get all your memories back. Your chord is the *full* moon – the gateway to all your memories. I'm sure that once you see it here, it'll all come back to you.' She smiled. 'And the next one is in just nine days.'

Winnibar opened the curtains to morning sunshine through a white frosted window.

Mandon grinned at Jayben. 'Let's get you home – back to the woods. You'll have the right medicine and be well again for whatever lies ahead. In the meantime, get some rest.' He began to herd everyone out. 'Let the boy recover,' he said.

As she walked past, Phee handed Jayben the star glass gem, glinting in the light. 'Another keepsake for your jar on the helicorn tree.' Then she passed him his Remindary. 'Here. We wrote down everything that happened the last few days. Just in case.'

Jayben opened it to see some fresh entries from his friends. It was hard to believe all that had really happened.

'Your turn to write the next page,' Phee said, handing him a pencil.

Jayben beamed. He felt warmer as they sailed back to the frozen harbour of Last Rock, returning by trox to the snowy Giantwood.

The mystery of his past was yet to be solved, his father was still missing and his future was far from certain, but now he had found the power inside. Now he believed in himself and that would get him to wherever he needed to go.

CHAPTER 29

Just The Beginning

Far away in the Earth World, a sleeping Ben Thomson began to stir.

The doorway between the two boys was beginning to open once more.

Jayben was sitting at the Fellers' kitchen table wearing a thick woolly jumper, happily sketching in the last rays of winter sun. It was one of many drawings he'd done in his Remindary over the past nine days, since returning to his friends in the forest. There were pictures of him whizzing down the long slide to

Ampelwed School, of snowball fights by the frozen lake, and one of them riding sledges down a hill, wearing Rackem helmets.

As he sketched the final strokes, he was distracted by a small twig from the table leg, tickling his shin with its leaves. 'Lottal!' he said with a giggle. He couldn't have been happier to be back with Tedrik's cheeky furniture. Back home.

Phee called out from the living room. 'Are you gonna help me hang this, or what?' she said, holding a long silver banner that spelled out:

HAPPY FULL MOON NIGHT!

Jayben grinned, putting his pencil down. Today was the day – the day he would finally see his chord properly and get all of his memories back.

'I didn't know there were more decorations!' he said, buzzing with excitement as they tied the banner beside the crackling fire. The sloping wooden beams of the house were still festooned with the gold beads and crimson bows from the winter Miraclest holiday. And now there were silver streamers too, and silver star ornaments.

'Here it is,' he heard Larnie say, coming downstairs

and handing him a much larger ornament of the moon. '*Now* it'll be perfect.'

He took hold of the moon and Larnie wandered out to the kitchen, cheerfully humming.

Jayben stood on a stool and, with a creak, its legs stretched until he could reach a hook on the wall. 'Thanks,' he said. Then suddenly he lost his grip and dropped the moon on his foot. To his surprise, he felt a sharp pain. '*Ouch!*'

'Ben?' said Phee, frowning.

Jayben froze. Pain could only mean one thing: that his crystals were going to switch him back to the Earth World. *No. Not tonight. Not full moon night.*

'I'm fine,' he said with a nervous laugh, quickly picking up the ornament and hanging it on the wall.

Phee said nothing and gave an unconvincing smile.

There was a muffled 'Oinff!' from the front door and it opened with a gust of frigid air.

'Brrrrr!' said Tedrik, stomping the snow off his heavy boots and ushering Peggro and Maybie inside.

Russog darted through, shaking the frost from his thick green fur, to stand by the warm fireside. 'You'll be sneezing snotsickles!' he said in Tedrik's voice.

Maybie giggled, unwinding her pink scarf. Then, of course, Russog let out a fart.

'Oi! Stinkbomb!' said Tedrik, closing the door. 'Away from the fire!'

'Wha-wha-what time,' Peggro shivered, 'are we g-g-going to the Jarmaster?'

Larnie appeared again, carrying a steaming mug to Tedrik labelled: *Never Mind Wine*. 'We'll eat first,' she said.

Tedrik winked at Jayben. 'We've got a wee something for you, lad,' he said, and from a sack he produced a large wrapped present. 'You would've had it for Miraclest last year.'

Jayben was so excited, crinkling the shiny blue paper in his hands. He knelt next to Russog and everyone gathered around.

'Open it, then!' said Phee, playfully nudging his shoulder.

He tore off the wrapping to unveil a midnight-blue backpack, his name embroidered in gold thread.

'For your next adventure,' said Larnie, putting her arm around him and pointing to the wooden toggles on the various compartments. They were fidgeting and one had a leaf sprouting from it.

'A few bits of home to keep with you,' said Tedrik, 'wherever you go.'

Jayben was speechless for a moment, overwhelmed

with gratitude. 'I love it!' he said, hugging the bag with a grin from ear to ear.

Maybie showed him there was a map of the Elf World rolled in a side pocket, with moving pictures, just like hers. Peggro pointed out a pouch where he could keep his compass. And Phee unfastened the top flap and joked, 'Now I don't always have to carry Russog.'

Suddenly there was a deep groan from the beams of the house and Russog scarpered to hide under an armchair. Jayben froze. Why would the house make that noise? His powers were steady now, he thought, absorbed by the crystal shilling, so they presented no danger. He quickly delved into his pocket to check the coin. Pulling it out, he gasped. It was opaque already. To absorb his power it needed to be transparent. His breathing quickened. Not only was he worried he was leaving Elf World again, but at the same time he could be about to cause another nightmare!

Larnie stood up and clapped her hands. 'Supper,' she said, as if nothing was wrong. 'Let's eat!'

Tedrik nodded, ruffling Jayben's hair. 'Tonight's the night!' he said, tapping the moon ornament as everyone followed Larnie.

Peggro whispered to his brother. 'But the coin. We need to tell Raynor.'

Jayben tried to reassure him, hoping to calm himself down too. 'It'll be okay. After tonight I might not need a shilling at all. When I get all my memories back, I'll control my powers, I bet.'

As he passed the oven he accidentally brushed his arm on a hot pan. '*Ah!*' he cried. It stung his skin. There was no denying it. He would soon be switching back to the Earth World.

He ran to the window, frantically wiping the condensation, hoping to spot the moon early. The sun was setting and the snowy woods twinkled with white glowing frostlight berries, but there was no sign of the moon yet. Where was it? He couldn't miss it. Not again. He needed his memories. He knew sometimes it came up before sundown. He only needed a glimpse . . .

'Not long now,' said Larnie, bringing him a damp towel. 'Let's see your arm. Poor little one.'

The table was piled high with delicious cheeses, fruits, biscuits and cakes. Everything was perfect. But then another noise disturbed him – a sound he had hoped he would never hear again: the ominous drumming of the trees.

They were sounding their alarm.

'You're gonna see the moon, Ben,' said Phee, nodding. 'Let's sit down, yeah?'

There was a knock at the door. 'Stay here,' said Tedrik with a furrowed brow, going to answer it.

The woods beat faster.

He opened the door and Mandon and Raynor hurried in.

'Jayben!' said Mandon. 'What happened?'

Tedrik laughed. 'The moon's not up yet. We'll all be ready soon. Come and help yourselves to something . . .'

Raynor shook her head. 'What's happened to the coin, Jayben?'

His heart sinking, Jayben showed them the murky crystal shilling. 'I don't know why it happened.'

Raynor took a step forward. 'Your power can no longer be contained by the shilling. Not now. Since the tomb, the boost to your Rainbow crystals from the star glass, it's become too great.'

'And your light,' said Mandon. 'It's brighter than ever! The Guards have seen it outside the woods. If we have, others will too. Coming into your powers is one thing, but until you've learnt to control them, it's not safe here any more.'

'We need to go,' said Raynor, taking Jayben's coat off the hook.

'What?' said Larnie. 'Where to?'

The drumming woods grew louder and the wind picked up, howling and swirling the snow, rattling the windows.

No, Jayben thought – this wasn't fair. He was so close to regaining all his memories. Besides, this was his home. 'But this is where I belong!' Jayben said, banging his fist on the table. 'Nowhere is safer than here.'

Raynor took a step forward. 'I understand. I do. But you know what your power is capable of.'

Jayben saw flashbacks of the tomb crumbling. The Rainbow crystals in Jayben's hand were flickering. He pulled out the crystal shilling again, and this time it cracked. Shocked, he dropped it on the floor. Then he looked back at the window, glowing orange in the sunset. 'But the full moon?' he said. 'My memories?'

'We'll make sure you see the moon,' said Mandon reassuringly. 'We need to go, Jayben. It's the only way to keep your family and friends safe.'

Jayben stood reluctantly. Phee darted to his side. 'I'm going with you.'

'Only Jayben,' said Raynor.

Then from the window there was a flash of darkness.

THUD!

Darkning. The house groaned loudly.

THUD! THUD!

It was coming closer. Russog started burping nervously, hiding under Larnie's legs.

'There must be another way,' said Larnie, putting her arm around Jayben.

'Yes,' said Tedrik. 'Another coin? A bigger one? Just tell me where to get one and I'll ride all night for it.' He turned to Jayben. 'It'll all be fine, lad. You've no need to go anywhere.'

Cruel as it was, Jayben had no choice. He grabbed his Remindary and drawings from the table and stuffed them into his new backpack, checking the Golden Torch and his compass in his pockets.

'No!' said Phee, grabbing him by the arm. 'You can't just leave us again already.'

Maybie agreed, with sad eyes. 'We missed you so much, Jay-Jay.'

'We still need to find Dad, remember?' said Peggro. 'We've faced darkning before. We can stick it out together.'

'This will be far worse,' said Mandon with a heavy

sigh. 'With the boost from the star glass. Stay here, Peggro. Where you'll be safe. Come, Jayben. I have your medicine. You'll be all right.'

THUD! THUD! THUD!

He suddenly felt heavy and extremely tired. The Rainbow crystals were glowing in his hand.

'It's going to be okay, Ben,' whispered Phee. 'You're going to see the moon.'

Tears filled his eyes. He could feel the burn on his arm stinging. 'Except I'm not,' he said, his voice faltering. 'I'm going to miss it again, Phee. I'm so sorry. I feel like I'm about to switch back. To the Earth World.'

Dimly, he heard the others talking. 'At least let *me* help,' Tedrik said.

'You're needed here,' said Raynor, taking Jayben's hat and scarf from the hook.

She opened the door to an icy blast. 'We'll go west. As far west as we can go, out of sight of any Agents, and somewhere the nightmares can't hurt anyone.'

Mandon buttoned Jayben's coat and led him outside.

His face stung in the bitter wind. His ears were ringing but he could hear the boots crunching on the snow. He saw a black closed carriage waiting for him down the path, and two grey trox thrashing their antlers in distress as the darkning strikes continued.

THUD! THUD!

He felt afraid and trapped and he slipped down in the snow. Tedrik scooped him up as Raynor opened the carriage, lying him on the seat, which was surprisingly warm. His legs and arms were numb. Looking back through the open door, he saw Phee, Peggro and Maybie standing outside the house.

Over the whistling wind he heard Phee shouting, '*Come back!*' But he couldn't respond.

Raynor closed the door from outside and Mandon sat beside Jayben, tucking him into a blanket and drawing a dark curtain that blocked out the sunset.

Resting his head on a pillow, Jayben felt the carriage jerk forward and he watched a swaying lamp on the ceiling above him as his vision blurred. He could feel the swirled end of the Torch against his leg, safely in his pocket.

'This is just the beginning,' said his grandpa, holding Jayben's hand as the Rainbow crystals shone brightly.

His eyes closed and his mind was pulled away to another world.

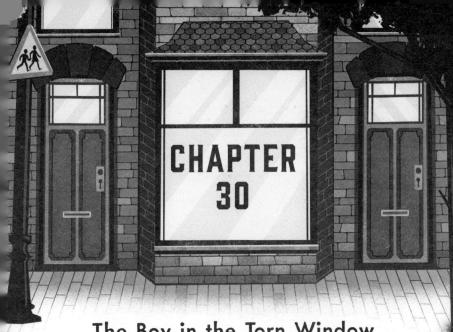

The Boy in the Torn Window

Ben opened his eyes to a dark room and the tiny squeak of a mouse. He heard the muffled sound of footsteps and he sat up with a start.

He looked around for Mandon – only Mandon wasn't there. Of course he wasn't. But still – *Ben could remember him!*

As extraordinary as it was, this time Ben knew exactly where he had been. Elf World. In Elf World he was Jayben, the Ninth Dreamer, and he had friends there – Phee and Peggro and Maybie. He had a home and a family who loved him.

But here in Earth World . . . he shivered. Here, his guardian was Null's earthling and Marcus was

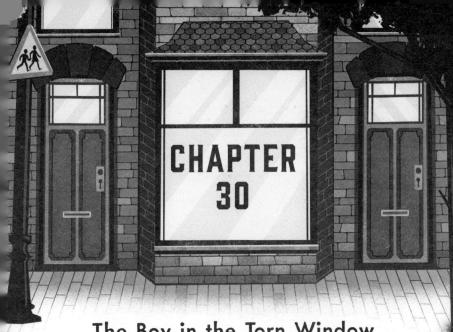

Zamar's. And Marcus knew about him.

He tried to gather himself. How long had he been away for? Last time it was only a few hours. Was it still Christmas Eve?

He was back in his gloomy bedroom in Samantha's house, on his hard, lumpy bed, still fully dressed in his blue coat. He switched on his bedside lamp to find his pet mouse nibbling on one of his drawings. 'Lucky!' he said, quickly scooping it into his hand. 'You need to stay hidden.'

The alarm clock read 4:15 p.m. He must have had a seizure. Had Samantha put him to bed? Where was she now?

Then he froze.

Would Samantha know she was Null's earthling? She wasn't a true Dreamer, so surely not. Or was that only people bitten by animals from Elf World, like Marcus? Either way, she was connected to Null.

There was a large red box on the floor, empty with no lid. Ben was sure he'd seen it before. He saw the rusty nail on the wall, by the patch of mould, and he realised – *the stocking*. He looked back at the box. The box had held Zamar's diamonds. And they were gone.

Marcus had taken them. The last year made sense

to Jayben now. All those little acts of supposed kindness . . . all that talk of helping Ben to achieve his dreams if they 'worked together' . . . and all the times he'd mentioned Ben having a 'remarkable gift' and insisting they not tell Samantha about his plan to help Ben . . .

'Just keep practising. You can do it. Then I'll get you whatever you want.'

He hadn't been talking about Ben's talent and dreams of becoming an architect; he'd been talking about Free-Dreaming. Marcus had witnessed Ben's powers before, over a year ago, after he was bitten by the hemnik.

He remembered Marcus standing in the sitting room just that morning, holding the stocking and grinning as Ben's power wreaked chaos. The hemnik bite on his hand had been smoking. Whatever magic was in it, it had connected Marcus with his elfling: Zamar. Marcus had tricked Ben and robbed him of the stocking, his most precious possession.

I should have known, he thought, seething with anger. He had swapped Terrisell's wand and the pencil back again, he remembered, so maybe, if he could get hold of those diamonds, he could Free-Dream the stocking back from the Elf World . . .

He heard the footsteps again, plodding downstairs, then Marcus's voice calling out 'Back in a bit!'

Ben leapt out of bed, putting Lucky gently in his coat pocket. He flung open the door and hurried down the stairs. 'Stop!' he shouted, as Marcus walked out into the rain with a large leather bag. Ben was certain it held the diamonds. 'Bring that back!'

Marcus opened his car door and turned to Ben with a grin. 'It's just business,' he said, quickly starting the car.

Before Ben could reach the front door a figure stepped forward and slammed it shut.

Samantha turned to face him. Her green eyes were sharp and she was scowling.

Ben felt a shiver down his spine.

Null.

'Back upstairs,' she said, almost whispering as she locked the door.

Did she know he was a Dreamer? Did she know that *she* was? Albeit not one of the true Dreamers of the Book. Ben wasn't sure. He hoped desperately she didn't realise her power. It was hard enough living with her, without her realising they were mortal enemies in another world.

'Just look what a mess you made,' she spat,

pointing into the sitting room. Ben could see the sofas were sodden, the walls dripping wet from where all the snow had melted. There were still pine cones on the floor and the broken clocks had been stacked up. 'I don't want to see your face for the rest of the holiday,' she snarled. 'Every time something goes wrong, here you are, the bane of my life. And if you think for one second that—' She stopped, looking down at one of his coat pockets, then made a sudden movement and snatched the piece of paper he'd shoved inside.

'Give that back!' he said. 'Please.'

Samantha held it up. It was his sketch of the festive department store, full of toys and books, and the smiling boy in the window on the top floor.

'Pathetic,' she sneered, before ripping it into pieces.

Ben felt his fury rising up, nostrils flaring, and in his mind he saw his Rainbow crystals sparkling.

Samantha tossed the torn pieces to the floor, tutting. 'Hopeless.'

No more.

Crack!

A bright flash of light and the banister of the stairs turned into a broad tree trunk, ripping through the floor and ceiling.

Samantha jumped, backing towards the kitchen.

Crack!

Another tree sprang up behind her, its branches waving.

The trees started drumming but Ben didn't flinch. He kept staring at his aunt.

Crack! Crack!

Another tree exploded from the wall, and another in the kitchen.

Samantha looked scared and raised her arms, as if trying to control it.

Crack! Crack! Crack!

More and more trees, bursting through the floor, drumming and clicking.

Samantha yelled at the trees, 'Stop this, at once!' But they kept coming, tearing the walls and ceiling of the house, the roots ripping through the kitchen tiles and smashing his aunt's immaculate flooring, until she was trapped, imprisoned by thick branches. 'Why isn't it stopping?' she screamed.

Ben didn't want to be here any longer. He gathered the pieces of his drawing from the floor. Then he stood up tall. He knew he was far too young to live alone, but there was no way he could go another day subjected to his aunt's cruelty.

Enough was enough. It was time to go. Somewhere. Anywhere but here.

With a deep breath, he opened the front door, looking back at his aunt through the trees.

'This is you, isn't it?' she cried. 'Like the wretched snow this morning. Get back here! Make it stop!'

Ben turned and ran out into the pouring rain, racing down the street, with no thought to where he was going, just so long as he was going away. He broke into giddy laughter, embracing the cold rain on his face. He was free. He couldn't believe it.

Every house he passed was twinkling with cheerful fairy lights and it reminded him of his school friend Emma. He knew he could count on her and her foster family. Emma was the one friend who had always listened to him and believed him when he told her about his home life. Emma had always said he could go to her if he needed to, so he ran all the way to their house.

Ben now sat on a comfy cream sofa, wrapped in a warm towel and blanket, beside a tree decorated with coloured lights. Carols were playing from a speaker as Emma walked in carrying two mugs of hot chocolate. She had long waves of flame-red hair, green eyes and rosy cheeks, and she wore a thick white sweater, knitted with a reindeer pattern.

'Better?' she said.

Ben was speechless. He'd never had a Christmas Eve anything like this before. Samantha would be livid! He grinned and gladly took the steaming cup of joy into his hands, while Lucky sat in his lap, chewing on a sunflower seed.

'Steph says she's got an old hamster cage that'll be perfect for Lucky,' said Emma.

'Thank you,' he said, taking a sip. 'This is amazing.'

Emma shrugged. 'It's Christmas, Ben. I'm sorry about your aunt. I got really lucky with this family. I'm so glad you can be here with us for a bit. Steph texted your aunt. Apparently she said it's okay for you to spend the night.' She passed him an enormous bowl of popcorn. 'Movie?' She switched on the TV. 'I'm going to find us something Christmassy.'

Ben smiled. On the one hand, this was perfect. On the other, it was hard to relax, knowing now that Samantha was Null, hell-bent on breaking the Golden Torch, draining both worlds of the Energy so that everyone could be controlled. At least she didn't know the truth for now.

Ben needed to get back to his friends in the Elf World, so he could find those missing pages from *The Book of Dreamers*, the words that would break the curse on the Golden Torch and light it for good. He knew to get back there he needed to see the dancing moon here – the other side of his chord. To see the full moon, distorted, like it was through the rainwater, appearing as it did in the Elf World.

Whatever the weather, rain or no rain, he'd find a way to distort it. Next month he would be ready . . .

He took out the ripped-up pieces of his drawing from his pocket and looked at the smiling face of the boy in the torn window. He recalled his aunt's words from that morning: *An architect? Don't make me laugh. You won't achieve anything in life. You are hopeless.*

But then he remembered the weird designs of the buildings in Karassan, and the lattice web of the krizzard, and the wild living beams of the *Beth Rose* – they were already inspiring new designs in his mind. And with the memory of the magical ship, he recalled words he'd been told at sea:

You won't need luck if you refuse to lose.

Ben knew that realising his dreams of becoming an architect wasn't going to be easy, but now he believed in himself. He'd seen that even when it seemed impossible, he could change his fate. One day he would be that boy in his picture – smiling and happy and safe. If he believed in himself, then it was just a matter of time.

'So, what did you want for Christmas?' asked Emma, settling on a classic festive film and dimming the lights.

'Oh,' he said, realising he hadn't dared to think about a present. What he really wanted couldn't be wrapped, but right now he was enjoying fitting into Emma's Christmas. 'Errr, ya know – stuff?'

'You're funny.' She smiled.

Ben noticed a wisp of smoke from a red advent candle. The wick had burned out, leaving a half-melted number '24' in the wax. In his mind he saw the Golden Torch once again.

'Wish this,' he whispered, and with a bright spark from the wick, the flame of the candle was back.

ACKNOWLEDGEMENTS

Thank you, dear reader, for joining me on this second leg of Jayben's adventure. I hope to see you again soon when Jayben returns.

Thank you to all the BRILLIANT kids I've met at so many fantastic schools and a big shout out to Leo (who gave me my first review) and Dylan in New Zealand, the marvellous Ruby, Nathan, Evie, Dulcie, Kira and Esther. And to Juniper whose superb pictures of the Golden Torch and hemniks have brightened up my writing desk.

This series would not be here without my fabulous agent Abi Fellows at DHH Literary Agency, Callen Martin, everyone at The Good Literary Agency and Polly Lyall-Grant – thank you!

I'm so very grateful to my wonderful editor Katie Lawrence and to everyone at Hachette Children's Group, especially Hilary Murray Hill, Emily Thomas,

Kristina Hill, Jennifer Alliston, Ruth Girmatsion, Joey Esdelle, Katherine Fox, Noah Grey, Nicola Goode, Jennifer Hudson, Emma Francini, Jemimah James, Annabel El-Karim, Valentina Fazio, Tracy Phillips, Zsofia Verhas and Jodie O'Toole. Thank you so much Genevieve Herr for all you've done and Teo Skaffa for once again bringing Jayben and his world to life with this stunning cover and beautiful map.

The biggest THANK YOU goes to my enormous family and the many great friends I'm so lucky to have in my life. Thanks to my parents, Jacqueline and Tony, my wife Sophie, and our children Phoebe and Lucy, for letting Daddy write sometimes and inspiring some of my favourite beings in the Elf World – 'Mee-mow!'

A special thanks to everyone who has supported Jayben since he set sail in the real world, in particular Beth Rose, Lee Newbury, Lizzie Huxley-Jones, Mahi Cheshire and all my fellow author pals. Thank you to the Epilepsy Society and Headway for your support. To Hamish Lloyd Barnes for doing such an amazing job at bringing this story to life in audio – you are the best! And a HUGE thank you to the fabulous Jacqueline, Vida and Tierney of Jacqson Diego Story Emporium, Virginia at Waterstones Southend, Lucy

May Lightning, Chicken and Frog Bookshop, and to all the brilliant booksellers working passionately to bring stories to readers.

Lastly, a tribute to my wonderful English tutor, Angela Myers, who gave so much to so many in her lifetime. Thank you for showing me the magic of a good story.

Thomas writes children's novels inspired
by his extraordinary life with a brain injury
and epilepsy. Having lost all his memories
in an accident, he rediscovered reading
and writing and was inspired to write an
adventure story after regaining a childhood
memory. He lives in Essex, making new
happy memories with his wife Sophie
and their two young children.